THREESOME

THREESOME

WHERE SEDUCTION, POWER AND BASKETBALL COLLIDE

BRENDA L. THOMAS

Writersandpoets.com, LLC

Publisher's Note:

This novel is a work of fiction. Any references to historical events;
to real people, living or dead; or to real locales are intended only to
give the fiction a setting in historic reality. Other names,
characters, places, and incidents either are the product of the
author's imagination or are used fictitiously, and their
resemblance, if any, to real-life counterparts is entirely
coincidental.

Writersandpoets.com, LLC
PO Box 496
Flourtown, PA 19031-0496

If ever there was an angel, my sister Gwen Brown was she.

July 1947 to December 1996

ACKNOWLEDGEMENTS

All Praises to Allah, Most Gracious, Most Merciful

I am blessed with more than just the ability to write. I am blessed to have known people to help me in this process of writing and self-publishing more than a book but a long-time dream. Throughout this process I have been overwhelmed by the love, prayers, support, phone calls, e-mails and guidance I have received. I must though acknowledge those who specifically contributed.

I would ask that my blessings go to the following people: Kelisha Rawlinson, my daughter and manager who's been with me on this journey; Kelvin Rawlinson, my son, here's hoping you get your drop top Benz; Horace Owens, my muse; Leigh & Bob Karsch, my friends and designer; my brothers, Joe, Gregory (who reminded me to hit my knees) and Jeffery Thomas; Tracy Diamond, who dusted off her editorial skills; Earl Cox, who helped me pull this off; Carmen Rodriquez-Carrion, my publicist; Kim Gerald, my sister-friend who pushed me and gave tough love; Barbara Campbell, my niece who always thinks I forget about her; Denise Robinson, who talked to me at least three times a day over the phone; and Maurice Carter, my future son-in-law. Thanks to my nieces, nephews, cousins, aunts, uncles and extended family, who spread the word, and my ancestors for building the foundation I now stand on.

And saving the best for last, I thank my parents Mary and Thurmond Thomas for reminding me to "Just be yourself Bones." And endless love goes to my granddaughters, Jazz, Briana, and Jada, the joy of my life.

If love were perfect, then it wouldn't be love.
B.L. Thomas

PROLOGUE

SASHA

MAY 1998

I thought I heard a noise downstairs, but figured it was just my imagination. No need to investigate – it was the same noise I always heard when I was here alone. Always thinking somebody might be sneaking into the house. I didn't have to worry tonight, though, because he was here with me. Maybe not for the whole night, but he would be here for a little while. His three, maybe four hours were usually enough to hold me over until the next time. And if someone did enter my home while he was here, then he'd be able to protect me, which is all I really wanted.

But there was the noise again. I lay there hoping it was the house settling, but I knew that this old house had long since settled. I turned to look at him; both of us had been unable to say anything since he'd come from inside me. Sometimes it was like that. Our lovemaking was so strong, so intense, that it took our words away, leaving us unable to talk about it until the next day. As I looked at him in amazement I heard the creaking of the stairs. Someone was definitely in the house. Before I knew it, she appeared in my bedroom doorway.

PAULETTE

I knew they were together tonight. I'd followed him there myself instead of having my cousin do it. I knew the house because I'd slowly driven by it on numerous occasions once I had all the evidence. Tonight I watched him ring the bell, instead of using his key. The lights were on downstairs, so I could make out through the slightly open blinds her greeting him with a kiss. Then I saw him sit at the kitchen table, and I sat motionless watching her shadow move about fixing his plate.

I'd always known he cheated, but I usually reasoned that all men did it, my husband being no exception. I knew he was busy, I mean with two jobs and his various community activities, he was always gone. Things were still the same at home though, the bills were paid and he treated us good but at times he just seemed happy about something that I wasn't part of.

I mean I had a busy life too. With my job, our son's activities and all the things I was involved in at church. I was often tired and distracted. I knew our marriage wasn't perfect, but it was solid. We had a comfortable home and were part of a decent community. I prayed he would return to church but he continued to profess to being Muslim. I didn't argue because at least he believed in God. My husband was always home for the holidays and each year he would agree to celebrate our wedding anniversary however I chose. But still I noticed.

Then our lovemaking changed. All of a sudden he didn't seem to mind when I didn't want to have sex and often I found myself having to initiate it. And why, I wondered, was he suggesting different things for dinner? Salads, fish, pasta, even dessert when it wasn't a holiday. All the time talking about being healthy, taking vitamins and going to the gym.

They were just little signs. Nothing obvious, like staying out all night. I mean once in a while he would come home late, at three or four in the morning, but it wasn't a big deal. What confused me the most was the *unobvious*. Did he or did he not smell slightly different? It wasn't another woman's perfume, just the faint scent of another woman's aura surrounding him.

Then he purchased a pager, and for a while he had a cell phone. I knew he talked to her on the phone at home because his facial expression showed it. I once tried to rig the answering machine to tape his calls, but it didn't work. I even attempted to follow him but gave up because I felt stupid and knew that if he noticed me, he would think I was crazy. So eventually I rationalized that I didn't have any real evidence and let it go.

Two years went by and even though his pattern didn't change, I knew he was slipping away. I found myself reading my Bible for answers, yet I would lie in bed full of anguish, scared to confront him. But I prayed and held fast that the Lord would work it out.

Finally, I needed to be certain. I went to my cousin and explained to him what had been happening. He seemed to know what to do. First he began following Cole, that's when he got her address and a picture. Then he had a friend who worked for Bell Atlantic come to our house and put a recording device in the phone. Two months later he came to me with the evidence. It was then that I took the package, went to my mother's house, where I wouldn't be interrupted, and there I listened – listened to my husband loving another woman.

COLE

After six months with her, I had to ask myself: What the hell was I doing? I knew that I'd gotten in too deep. When I'd met her I thought she might be fun for a while, like the others had been. Hell, she was single and had her own crib on the other side of town. Just what I needed. I met her driving by on the street. I was walking towards my truck and she was driving past me in her Honda Accord when our eyes met. I mean I'd caught the eyes of a lot of women on the street but something was different about those eyes.

I motioned for her to pull over and she did, but before I could even turn towards her car, she pulled off again. I figured what the hell, jumped into my Suburban and began driving down Broad Street. After only a few blocks I saw her making a U-turn in the gas station, I blew my horn and motioned for her to pull over. This time she parked and I knew the shit was on.

When she stepped out her car in a brown linen suit I was impressed with how tall, slender and brown she was. Not my usual pick of women, who are light-skinned, with long hair and built like shit. No, her hair was natural, full of kinky locs and she had this look of freedom to her. A little makeup maybe but I really couldn't tell 'cause I kept looking at her smile. Once we introduced ourselves I could feel my dick start to get hard. Damn, she was fine.

We found a lot to talk about, except for the fact that I was married. I wasn't about to reveal that, not before I at least had a chance to hit that thing. So we rapped for about an hour, more than I usually did with a strange woman and then she climbed back into her car. As I leaned into the passenger window, she gave me her business card and it was then that I noticed her sliding her long sexy foot out of a brown leather mule. Now, I'd always had a foot fetish; shit, I had over one hundred pairs of shoes and probably even more sneaks. But this foot was beautiful and I was anxious to get those toes in my mouth.

I put her card carefully in my pocket, knowing that Sasha was gonna make my August hotter than my July had ever been.

SASHA

For the first year I didn't even know he was married. A relationship and falling in love were the furthest things from my mind. I'd just gotten out of a relationship three months before I met him, so all I wanted was someone to take the edge off.

My career was moving on fast-forward as I'd just gone from being secretary, to a college dean, to an executive assistant at the high-powered Philadelphia law firm of Mitchell & Ness, whose clients were entertainers and athletes. So I was too busy to realize when he wasn't available. Shit, I couldn't help but be attracted to him. He stood 6'4" tall, with a thick 240 pounds spread evenly over him. But more than that, it was the deep black color of his skin that mesmerized me.

Once I found out Cole was married I was simply too caught up to let him go. I'd tried to end it several times, but each time I was pulled back, with him offering me just enough to keep me right there. I often grew tired of living our relationship inside my house and out of state, when he could get away. I wanted us to be normal and he wanted me to be patient. But nothing could take away those lonely Sunday nights when I'd listen to WDAS FM play ...*Outside Woman, Saving My Love, Agony and Ecstasy, Secret Lover...*, all the songs that described our relationship.

He kept telling me his wife didn't know anything, didn't even suspect. Having been a wife myself I found that hard to believe, but he insisted. So I figured she was either dumb or didn't care;

hell, maybe she had her own thing on the side. Regardless, he was totally unwilling to let me go, yet he was also unwilling to leave his wife. Which I'm not even sure I wanted him to do. I didn't want to see him or his family suffer, so instead I endured the suffering.

PAULETTE

It would be easy getting into her house. I'd copied her keys from the extra ring he kept on his key chain.

I took the gun off the seat beside me and carefully placed it in my pocketbook. I looked around before I stepped out the car and then glanced up to her window to make sure nobody saw me coming. I didn't care that I'd used my own car, nor that I'd parked directly across the street from her house. In the end none of that would matter. The best part was that he had no idea that I knew he was sharing his love with another woman.

As I said a prayer, in an effort to decide if tonight would be my night, the lights went out downstairs, and what appeared to be candlelight began flickering in the bedroom. I hesitated, as the aching in my heart made me want to pound on her door to be let inside. To be let back into the life he'd shut me out of. But no, tonight I would make my move.

I walked past his truck parked in her driveway and onto the porch. Holding the screen door open I slowly inserted the key; I tried the top lock first but it wasn't locked so I used the doorknob key – it opened. My hands were shaking and I felt sweat beading up between my breasts – I was even more determined. I turned the knob and stepped inside.

I was surprised by the house's simplicity. There were dark stained hardwood floors that ran throughout the downstairs. The living and dining rooms were covered with Oriental rugs that I'm sure were expensive. I could smell her scent of jasmine and spice and unexpectantly I was immediately drawn into Sasha's strange aura, as it had probably drawn in my husband. Yes, I'm sure she had used all of these things to lure my husband away. She was no better than Eve, who had tempted Adam.

The house was quiet except for the television, and then I heard it, the sound of my husband snoring. For 14 years I'd listened to that breathing and light choking when he sucked in air too deeply. I started towards the stairs but then changed my mind; no, first I wanted to see how she lived. See where he was so comfortable over these last five years that he didn't want to be in our home, except to pass through, as if I were the other woman. Why hadn't he ever told me about her, told me he loved someone else, that he wanted a divorce? No, he just silently kept living two lives. I had to stop myself from thinking too much, so I silently prayed.

Her house, even though simple, was tastefully furnished. I sat down on a chair in the living room, facing a large-screened television, which I'm sure was his favorite spot and I guessed that it was probably here that she sat between his legs. But I couldn't get caught up in that, not right now. There were also plants that filled her home, and fresh flowers that stood on a pedestal. And there were pictures of her grandson.

Then I went into the kitchen. This is where she probably pleased him most. My husband loved to eat and I could tell from the smell that she had been baking. There were dishes on the counter, still covered with food: chicken smothered in gravy, rice, salad and even a fresh baked apple pie on the counter. I couldn't help but wonder if her food tasted better than mine, so with my fingers I picked a piece of chicken out of the cold gravy and tasted it. Dirty dishes and leftovers, that's how I felt, like a meal he was finished with but couldn't seem to throw away – well, now he'd have no choice.

I walked back through the dining room, living room and, hesitating at the bottom step, looked up to where all my anguish was coming from. Again, I prayed. As I put my foot on the first step, it squeaked. I held my breath but realizing it was too late to turn back, I proceeded, one step at a time.

I knew her room was in the front of the house. So once I reached the top step, I held onto the banister to brace myself. More family pictures on the wall and then on the table in the hallway there sat a picture of the two of them – laughing and happy. Even though my body cringed, I had to admit they even looked in love. But that was my love, my love she'd stolen.

Then I felt it. I felt her sense me, like she knew I'd come. But what she didn't know was what I'd come for. I took the gun from my purse and positioned it firmly in my right hand, removed the safety and placed my finger on the trigger. God will forgive me I told myself.

Initially I wasn't going to say anything, just do it, but I wanted them to see it happening, and not have a chance to stop me. Approaching the doorway I froze at the sight of the two of them, all cozy and tucked in bed. I wanted to turn away, but no I was doing the right thing. Hadn't I prayed for this night?

What better way for them to pay? They'd hurt me for so long, and Cole actually thought he was getting away with something. Did he really think I didn't know? For once I would no longer be the good girl, it was my turn to be bad.

COLE

Damn, it felt good to be in bed with her. She had no idea how bad I wished I could just up and leave my family. But no matter how much I thought it through I still came out with the same answer. It was too much work, I had too much to lose. I couldn't walk out on my son, or my wife. Even though our marriage didn't hold any excitement, I still loved Paulette and didn't want to see her hurt. Shit, I even wondered how after all these years she still didn't know. But guess what, I wasn't gonna try to figure it out either. If Paulette could only give me half of what Sasha did, then maybe it would be different at home.

I truly believed Sasha loved me. She knew how to take care her man. Whatever I needed she'd give to me. Backrubs, baths, dinner on the table when I arrived, TV turned to ESPN, slippers by the door and sex, well I got that any and every way I wanted it. Sometimes it wasn't even the sex, it was just the way she seemed genuinely interested in my life. She believed I could do some of the things I'd lost faith in doing. She was so damn interesting to me; the athletes and celebrities she knew from her job and all that shit she liked; candles, reading, writing and all that back-to-nature stuff. Sasha wasn't scared of shit. If there was something she wanted to do or try she'd go after it. She had no problem taking risks; hell, I was a risk.

I'd had a lot of women over the years, before and during my marriage but once me and Sasha hooked up I knew she had me because I hadn't fucked with anybody else. Even though I told her

I didn't sleep with my wife, I knew she didn't believe me, but what else could I say? But the sex wasn't the same; lovemaking with Paulette was the same as our marriage – routine. Sasha made me feel like a man. She not only loved me but she loved my body and would examine and make love to every inch of it, even down to my crusty toes. So what was I gonna do – give all this up?

Having Sasha was better than having a wife. 'Cause I knew after being with my wife for 14 years that wives didn't give that much. They just gave enough to stay married. That's why I also knew that as much as she wanted me here, if I were to come, to move in, she would change. She'd get comfortable and feel like she didn't have to treat me special anymore. As long as the relationship stayed like this, I could be with her forever and then maybe one day, when my son graduated high school I could make a move. And she knew; she knew I wasn't leaving and didn't often ask except those times when she wanted me so bad she couldn't take it anymore. I knew I was selfish but the way things were is what worked for me.

Sasha did deserve more – deserved a man that could be there with her in the morning and be able to count on him coming home every night, someone she could feel like number one with. But what she didn't know is that she was number one with me. I couldn't let her go, I couldn't let her give anybody else what she'd given me. So lying here tonight, after having been drenched in her love, I was in my comfort zone. The way she laid tucked underneath me like a finished puzzle, made me know that she felt the same way.

SASHA

I knew she'd come. No matter how much he denied she had knowledge of us, I knew eventually she would let us know she was no real fool. So here we were, the three of us. Even with the gun in her hand we just stared at each other, knowing it had come to this. I could see through the dimness of the evening light, that Paulette was sadly beautiful.

Who would she shoot, Cole or me? Who would she hold to blame, Cole because he was her husband, the one who'd stood before God and made the commitment? Or me because she thought I was some whore breaking up their marriage? I still couldn't move. I called Cole's name, watched his body slowly turn, saw his face look at her, look at me and before I could answer the question in his eyes…

COLE

I know Sasha thought I was sleeping, but her squirming had already woke me, so when she called my name I didn't answer right away. Then I felt Sasha nudge me and I heard my name being called again but this time it was my wife's voice. I turned over to make sure I was hearing right and there she stood. What the fuck was my wife doing in Sasha's bedroom doorway?

As my eyes adjusted to the darkness I could see that not only was my wife there but she was holding my fucking 9-millimeter in her hand. I looked from Sasha to Paulette to ask what the fuck was going on, but before I could say anything, before I could even explain, as if there would be an explanation why I was in another woman's bed, the gun went off.

PAULETTE

Sasha and I never took our eyes off each other while she called his name, and when he didn't respond, I called him. He moved, he turned, looked at me, looked at her and before he could ask any questions, I pulled the trigger.

CHAPTER 1

CRIME SCENE
MAY 1998

Before Cole could get out of bed he had to slap me to stop my screaming. Paulette had shot herself at close range through the head. He grabbed my face tightly, pushed the phone in my hand and shouted for me to call 911. I dialed the number while Cole fell to the floor cradling Paulette's body, as if he could push the pieces of her back together.

The police dispatcher tried to keep me rational by asking numerous questions. Tears filled my eyes as I tried to explain.

"What's your name ma'am?
"Sasha Borianni."
Where do you live?" she asked.
I gave her my address.
"Ms. Borianni is the person still breathing?"
"I don't know," I answered, even though my instincts told me Paulette was dead.
"How long ago did it happen?"
I noticed my watch on the nightstand and fastened it to my arm.
"Damn it, it just happened!" I yelled, tears choking my throat.
"Is the scene safe?" she asked in a very monotone voice.
"Yea." I could feel myself fading away.
"Who shot her?" she asked.
"She did it." I whispered.

"I don't understand? Is the gun still there?" She hesitated, waiting for my reply.

"Ma'am, do you know the victim?"

Did I? I silently wondered.

Frustrated with her questions. I cried. "Could you just please hurry up and send some help?"

I hung up the phone realizing that I had to phone Amir, Cole's brother, which had always been his instructions if anything ever happened. While I explained the story of Paulette's suicide, Amir remained quiet and only asked where his brother was.

Within minutes I saw flashing red lights reflecting off my windows and heard sirens rushing towards my home, simultaneously the doorbell rang. Realizing I was naked, I pulled on Cole's tee shirt that was lying on the floor. I ran to the door where two policemen identified themselves and asked what happened. I could see an ambulance and paramedics running up the driveway and police cars coming from both ends of my one-way street.

"Who's here with you?" The White officer asked while peering at my half-naked body.

"Me and Cole." I answered, as if he knew us.

"Is it safe to come in the house?"

I shook my head yes and pointed upstairs. "He's with her, he's holding her."

At this point his Puerto Rican partner spoke into his radio repeating various code names and numbers but it was clear he was contacting the Homicide Division.

The White officer asked, while opening his notebook. "What's your full name Ma'am?"

"Sasha Borianni."

"And the man's name?"

"Cole Allen."

"His wife?"

"Paulette Allen."

Unsure of the circumstances, the cop had me follow him up the steps to my bedroom. Holding the cordless phone, I stood in the hallway, while two officers and the paramedics who had entered the house trailed us. The cops cautiously entered my bedroom being careful not to disturb anything. One cop slowly moved towards Cole and eased Paulette from his arms while the other officer bent down to check the pulse in Paulette's neck and wrist. The look they gave each other confirmed that she was dead. The paramedics began helplessly trying to resuscitate Paulette, I guess because it was their job to at least try. But their efforts were wasted and within minutes they pronounced her dead. Cole just sat on the floor staring right through all that was happening.

Before I could go to Cole, a detective came through the doorway and introduced himself as Detective Rankins from the Homicide Division and his partner, a woman no less, as Detective Stiles. I could tell right by the way she looked me over that Detective Stiles detested me. I looked at her hand and noticed that she was married and I knew why. As Rankins looked me up and down, in my state of half-nakedness, he asked me if I'd like to put some clothes on, which seemed to piss Stiles off. Unable to speak, I shook my head yes. I pulled my sweatpants from the floor where Cole had just hours ago stripped them from me. Stiles motioned for me to follow her into the bathroom as she eerily watched me get dressed.

However, before I could finish, someone yelled from my bedroom.

"Yo Stiles, we need some help in here!"

I ran behind Stiles to my room where Cole, still naked, was bending over his wife's body, whom the coroner was inspecting like a dead animal. I noticed they'd covered their shoes with plastic booties and inserted Paulette's hands into brown paper bags. I also noticed they'd placed the gun into a plastic bag. Cole was splattered with blood from his thighs to his waist. Two officers were practically dragging him out the room and down the hallway. I began to get angry, "Can he at least get some clothes on?" I asked.

"Sure Ma'am," Rankins said.

"Well, they're on the chair in my room!"

Another officer passed me the clothes as they led Cole downstairs, followed by Rankins in front and Stiles behind us.

Once they had Cole downstairs, sitting in what was his favorite chair, I went to him but he turned away from me and Rankins told me it was best if I stayed in the other room. I could tell they were trying to keep us apart, but I couldn't figure out why. I assumed they thought we had a different story to tell, but it didn't matter because Cole wasn't talking. I stood watching Cole from the kitchen doorway, a broken man. His entire body was limp and he wasn't even able to hold his head up. Never having seen him cry, I watched tears stream from his eyes, as over and over he repeated, "Allah, what have I done?"

The next official people to come through the door was the crime lab. Detective Rankins went back upstairs and gave orders that it was okay to enter the *crime scene*. A chill shot through my body like somebody had dropped crushed ice through my veins and I began to shake. I could hear the officers talking about *sifting through evidence* and *collecting fibers* and everything began to get clear.

There were so many policemen and detectives in the house that I felt like I'd stepped into a movie. They had filled my home and quickly cordoned off my bedroom with yellow tape that read "crime scene" in black letters. I could hear the cops outside talking to the one's in the house on walkie-talkies, *trying to secure the scene.* Everyone knew their role, as one officer took pictures and another spoke into a tape recorder, giving details of what was now officially the *crime scene.*

I found myself obsessed with checking my watch for the time, it was 11:00 pm. It couldn't have been more than an hour since I'd first called 911. I watched and listened as they brought down bags of evidence and took them outside to the *black-and-white crime scene vehicle.* Paulette's body still remained and from what I overheard one of them say, "she'll be the last thing to go because the coroner hasn't finished yet."

But still I wanted to be strong, hold onto some dignity with all these strangers in my house. It was then that Stiles spoke up and announced that we'd have to go downtown to give a statement.

Rankins and Stiles then began hustling Cole and I along, to separate cars, taking us to Police Headquarters, at 8th and Race Streets. When they escorted us outside I noticed that the television news vans had showed up. But the police were holding them back because they'd marked my house off with barricades. I also noticed that Amir was waiting. They hadn't allowed him to enter the house. I told Rankins who he was and he sent an officer to tell Amir to meet us at the Roundhouse.

My life had now become a spectacle for all. I had nothing to shield my face from the onlookers so I just kept my head down, however in doing that I noticed that someone had trampled my recently sprouted flower-bed of pansies and tulips lining the driveway.

Arriving at the Roundhouse, we found Cole's mother and attorney waiting. Cole's mother charged toward me, filled with rage, as if I were the one who'd pulled the trigger. But before she could reach me, Amir grabbed her arm and led her away but I still heard her hateful words, "Bitch, look what you've done, you've killed my son's wife!"

I felt Rankins' eyes on me, and without looking at his face, I could tell he pitied me. Maybe he thought I'd killed Paulette to get Cole. But no he'd been nice to me and seemed to believe everything I'd told him. It was Stiles and the other cops who had snooped around through things that had nothing to do with what had happened. They had poked into what I thought was a relationship but would now be known as nothing more that a sordid affair.

My strength was waning because I knew that what she said was true. My selfishness and greedy need to love Paulette's husband had surely pushed her over the edge and caused her death. If only I'd alerted Cole when I'd first heard the noise, maybe Paulette would still be alive. I needed to call somebody. I couldn't do this alone. So I asked to phone my attorney, not that I had one but I knew Mitchell, the entertainment lawyer I worked for, would come to the station. At this request Stiles in her bitchiest voice asked, "Now why would you wanna do that? You guilty of something?" I knew it was better to keep my mouth shut because she had me at her mercy but instead Rankins spoke up. "Leave her alone Stiles."

It took Mitchell an hour to get there and fortunately they gave us some time alone. He'd met Cole on numerous occasions but had no idea that he was a married man. After telling him what happened I asked him to call the three people who were closest to me; my son Owen in California, my Daddy, and my best friend Arshell who lived in Maryland.

Then the questioning began. "Now, Ms. Borianni can you please tell me again the *chain of events*?" All of a sudden things had taken on new names. I hesitated at first, thinking of my rights but realizing I hadn't shot anyone, I told him how Paulette had appeared in my bedroom doorway.

"What time did you first hear the noise?" asked Rankins.

"Why didn't you wake Mr. Allen? How long have you two been having an affair?" Chimed in Stiles before I could answer the first question.

Rankins continued, "What time did it happen? What were you doing at the time?"

All of a sudden Rankins didn't seem to be so nice anymore.

"Did she see you having sex?" Stiles kept digging. "C'mon Ms. Borianni, I'm sure you realized that it would be much easier for you and Mr. Allen to be together with his wife out the way."

Then it was Rankins turn. "You really want me to believe that you didn't want Ms. Allen out the way?"

My emotions were boiling over – I stuttered in answering their questions because they were coming too fast. I screamed. "She committed suicide, can't you fuckin' tell!"

Then Mitchell spoke up, "Excuse me detectives, but if you're not charging my client with anything then I ask that she be free to go."

I thought to myself, "maybe this was just a movie I was caught in."

After six hours of their grueling questions and checks into my background I was finally free to go. As much as I wanted to keep my head up, my eyes were burning from crying, along with the sun beating down on me as we walked to Mitchell's car.

Arriving back at my house, there were still a few police cars and reporters lurking about. I could see my neighbors standing on their front lawns talking with each other and I was sure the cops had questioned them, since many of them had met Cole and seen him come and go over the last five years. The people of Chestnut Hill certainly weren't used to the publicity they were being exposed to. I had tainted my neighborhood's cobblestone streets and quaint shops with blood.

Inside the house, Daddy sat on the couch fidgeting with the TV remote control, unable to even find the power button. I'd never seen him like that. He didn't say much just motioned for me to sit next to him. Mitchell explained in detail what had occurred and I watched as creases formed across Daddy's forehead.

"What do we need to do Mitchell?" Daddy asked.

"Just hold tight, I have a friend who can probably handle this."

"What's there to handle? She killed herself, right?" He asked, glancing at me for reassurance. Mitchell didn't wait for me to respond.

"Yes, but they'll want to investigate some more to make sure there was no foul play and I just want to make sure Sasha's rights are protected."

Through the screen door I noticed a cab pulling up carrying Owen, who'd obviously taken the Red Eye flight from Los Angeles. He ignored reporters, nosy neighbors and police. I stepped into the doorway to meet him and Owen immediately took me in his young arms. "Mom, what happened?" He'd known about Cole for the last few years and had been on me to leave him alone as he insisted that I'd deserved more – but now I reasoned in my head that I was probably getting what I deserved.

"Owen, I'm sorry, it wasn't my fault." I cried.

My mind was drained and my body beaten. So we sat in the kitchen, me, Mitchell and Owen, nobody knowing the right words to say. Mitchell went through the story again but I could tell Owen wanted to hear from me. However, everytime I tried to talk, tried to make it right, make some sense out of the nightmare I was living, tears choked the words out of me. So I gave up.

Mitchell made a few phone calls and then announced he was leaving. I walked him to the door apologizing and thanking him at the same time. Outside I noticed that everyone had gone and the streets where children usually played were empty.

The house grew quiet, with my father lying on the couch while Owen stood washing the dishes and scraping away me and Cole's leftovers. Finally I found the courage to ask him to go upstairs with me. I had to see.

From the end of the hallway I could see the chalk outline of where Paulette's body had been. Then there was the blood, it had touched everything. It wasn't just on my hardwood floors, but had splattered on my soft yellow walls and bedding. There was debris scattered around the room from their investigation. Multiple pairs of rubber gloves the police had used in examining her and paper and plastic wrappers from the different instruments. "Why didn't the police clean up?" I asked Owen. He didn't bother to answer, just stepped into the bedroom and looked around, with me following close behind. "Mom, I'll clean it up," he said. But I couldn't move, I leaned against the wall and stared at the shape of her, wondering about the type of person she'd been. Cole and I rarely discussed her. Then it hit me – Cole's son had also lost his mother. What had I done? Maybe I had killed her. At that moment I wanted her to return to my doorway so I could apologize for loving her husband.

I hadn't noticed that Owen had left the room until I saw him return with a mop, sponges and a bucket filled with hot water and Lysol. He kept insisting that I go downstairs so he could clean up. I ignored him and reached into the bucket, squeezed out the mop and began mopping up her blood, while Owen took a sponge and started cleaning the blood speckles off the walls. As I put the mop back into the bucket, I watched the water turn pink and I began to cry, just a few tears at first and then racking sobs – I was so distraught Owen had to grab me because my legs were buckling. It felt like my bones were detaching from each other, my knees hit the floor and I fell, fell down into her blood that was now mixed with water and tears. Through my blurred eyes, I could see that not only was her blood on the floor but brown pieces of what had probably been Paulette were also there.

"No, no!" I screamed. "This can't be happening! Why couldn't she have killed me? I was the one who deserved to die. Cole I'm so sorry."

I was so hysterical that Owen yelled for his grandfather. The two of them picked me up and laid me in bed, which only made it worse because I could smell Cole and the scent of our sex from just hours before.

Owen begged, "Mom, please don't do this to yourself."

"Sasha, Sasha!" My father screamed, trying to get through to me.

Then I heard Arshell calling my name, she had come in the house and was running up the stairs. She ran into the room, moving Owen and Daddy out of the way to reach me. Arshell ordered Owen to get a glass of water, pulled a container of pills from her purse, told me to open my mouth and inserted two Xanax's. "I can't lay here, please, Arshell, I can still smell them. She's still here."

"Nobody's here, Sasha, but your family."

"Arshell, it's all my fault," I kept repeating, as she held me and rocked me until I finally fell into a fitful sleep.

The next morning I woke up horrified that I'd fallen asleep in my room. At first I wasn't even sure what day it was but looking at my watch I saw it was 10:00 in the morning. Lying beside me was Owen. Even in sleep I could see that my son felt powerless over the lifestyle his mother had chosen to live.

I climbed out of bed and saw that the blood had been cleaned up, but I could still smell it, Paulette's suicide smelled like raw chicken gone bad. I went to the bathroom where I coughed and gagged trying to throw up but nothing came out, so I sat on the side of the tub, turned on the water, but didn't have the strength to take a shower. I yearned for Cole at that very moment. I needed him to make me understand what had happened in the last two days. Knowing he was farther out of my grasp then he'd ever been I instead pulled on my bathrobe, a present from Cole, and went downstairs to the comforting sound of Arshell's voice. She was hanging up the phone as I entered the kitchen.

"Listen, Mitchell called, he's getting you a criminal attorney."

"What do I need a lawyer for? I didn't do anything."

"Look Sasha, this is what you have to understand. The cops know it was a suicide, but they could easily switch this shit up and blame it on you and Cole."

Arshell turned away from me but I noticed from the movement of her shoulders that she was crying. I went to her, wrapping my arms around her waist and there we stood, the both of us, weeping over the affair that had ended Paulette's life.

"And Sasha, there's more."

"What is it?" I asked, not even sure I wanted to know.

"You can't talk to Cole," she said, almost in a whisper.

"What? What do you mean?" I dropped my arms from around her and she turned to face me.

"You are not to see him. You are not to talk to him until this shit is over, so don't try any dumb shit. You hear me?"

I finally understood. Not only had Paulette taken her own life, but she'd taken mine too.

CHAPTER 2

ROOTS
JUNE 1998

As the days passed and everyone returned to their lives, Arshell to Maryland and Owen to California, my life strayed farther and farther from normal. It seemed everywhere I went in Philly people stared at me, like they knew I was a dirty whore who'd slept with a married man, whose wife had killed herself. The local news kept the scandal and relationship alive long after it stopped breathing. I'd even received threatening phone calls from supposedly "church sisters" of Paulette's. Too many nights I cried on the phone to Arshell about my horrible existence.

Most every morning I was awakened by images of Paulette laughing at me. I'd taken to sleeping on the futon in my sun porch, where Cole and I had spent many summer evenings, because I couldn't bring myself to return to my bedroom. On these nights I would sit up reading the diary my long ago deceased mother had written while she was pregnant with me. Most of it was abstract sentences, but she had definitely been happy to be pregnant. She hadn't known whether I'd be a boy or girl, but she'd intended on loving me and teaching me strong values. Daddy didn't like to talk about my mother much but reminded me that she died giving birth to me. Which I think made me feel more guilty than anything else.

Judging by my current circumstances, I guessed I needed those lessons. Not that Daddy hadn't tried, but he was certainly lacking in emotional availability. However, there were things that Daddy had given to me. Even though it was just the two of us Daddy made me feel like we were a complete family. Daddy said there had been a lot of nay-sayers when Mommy died who said he couldn't take care of a baby or raise a little girl by himself but he was determined to prove them wrong.

Mealtime was important to Daddy as it was usually here when he would talk about my mother. He would tell me how patient she'd always been with him, yet when she wanted her way she would make her demands leaving him no recourse but to say yes.

Even then Daddy still missed her cooking so he began to teach me at age 10 how to fry chicken and make potato salad, two staples he said a Black woman must always know how to cook. When his memories of my mother would overwhelm him, because I never got enough, he'd just say, "Well, Sasha, it's just me and you now."

I always felt like Daddy's little princess and I know he gave me extra love because I was all he had. I was the only woman he could trust he said. Daddy, as he insisted I always refer to him, made it known that when I became a woman I was never to call another man by that name, that he was the only man worthy of that title.

Daddy was employed as a limousine driver and I spent a lot of time riding quietly in the front seat while he drove people with money around to places we never entered. He was always explaining the importance of money and the things it could buy. At Christmas there were boxes of clothes and toys that I hadn't even asked for. On Valentine's Day there were hearts filled with chocolate and always a jewelry trinket. His gifts weren't expensive but he needed a way to show his love.

His grandmother had been a full-blooded Italian of which he held little resemblance but made sure I knew my heritage. Daddy didn't know a lot about Italy but he knew a helluva lot about the Mafia, even if most of it was from television. He owned the entire Godfather series and any other movie that carried a mob storyline. I grew up between North Philly and West Philly where there weren't a lot of Italians but there was a lot of Black culture.

But there was another side of him. Daddy enjoyed gambling. He wasn't obsessed but he loved a good card game and was always comparing life and its events to a deck of cards. Most especially he often repeated, "Sasha, don't ever let anybody see your full hand."

Growing up he constantly told me I had to be tough, to be strong, that I couldn't be soft like most women. When I complained about not having a mother, he would reply, "You can't miss what you never had." But I did, even though I pretended it didn't bother me – especially when I'd see other little girls dressed up with their mothers fussing over them. I had no idea what it felt like to call somebody Mommy, and would often practice those words in the mirror, like if I said them hard enough and long enough she might appear. No matter how long I practiced, she never came.

When Daddy did go out, I'd spend that time with my mother's sister, who was good to me but couldn't be good herself. I hated my Aunt Lou for continually allowing herself to be abused by Ernest, her no-good funky smelling boyfriend. When I would spend the night, I'd listen to her cries as she was beaten and then forced to have sex. I couldn't understand why one moment she'd be screaming at him to stop hitting her and then the next she'd be moaning in pleasure. As always, the following morning she'd school me on how men had problems and needed to be understood. All I understood at the time was that sex was used to somehow make pain disappear, just the same I suppose as a kiss made a child's bruises feel better. Maybe it was the same with adults?

According to Daddy, Sasha meant "protector of men," and he constantly reminded me that I had to protect him. It was my job to protect Daddy from his women getting too close. He never let another woman live with us – they barely spent the night and I certainly kept them out of our kitchen.

Daddy thought that I needed to know how to be a good woman to a man and how not to let one take advantage of me. "They gotta pay the cost to be the boss," he'd say, when I'd talk to him about boys. He insisted that a man should always have something to offer me because what they wanted in return was too precious to give away.

But women and money were what satisfied Daddy, I realized early on that sex was a priority for men. He would bring women home often after I'd gone to bed, and sex seemed to always make those women happy. I wanted that happiness. I would sometimes peak downstairs and watch him have sex. I couldn't believe that a woman could make my Daddy look weak. They did things to him that, at the time, I thought were disgusting. But afterwards he'd return to the same strong man I always thought he was. Like he had no idea that he'd just been in another place. I envied that a woman could control a man with sex and vowed that one day I would possess that same control.

CHAPTER 3

ROOKIE
AUGUST 1998

It had been almost five months since the tragedy and there was the lingering possibility of a civil trial. Paulette's family was suing me and Cole in civil court. The charge was "intentional infliction of emotional distress – wrongful death." There were several meetings between me and my criminal attorney, Joel Senquinni, who needed to know all the details of my relationship with Cole. There was also the issue of custody – Paulette's mother was fighting with Cole for his son. And from what I heard, Cole Jr. wanted to be with his grandmother.

I hadn't returned to work so the only activity I had was my volunteer work at the Morris Arboretum. Mitchell, to finally lure me out my shame and back to work, decided to present me with what he called "the opportunity of a lifetime." It seemed one of Mitchell's clients, a 23-year-old, NBA All Star, named Phoenix Carter who played center for Chicago, was in need of a personal assistant. I vaguely knew Phoenix through a few phone conversations while waiting for Mitchell to pick up, but for the most part I kept my distance from all the celebrity clients.

I didn't want to get too excited, but it did sound interesting. Mitchell informed me that Phoenix would be phoning me later in the week so we could set up a meeting to discuss the details. He wanted to get everything settled before the season opened in

November. From the sound of things, it looked like I didn't have a choice because Mitchell and Phoenix had already decided my new life for me.

It was a Thursday morning when Phoenix phoned and I made reservations at The Striped Bass for the three of us. Driving in the 92° Philly humidity I cursed myself for not getting the air conditioner in my car repaired. But my mechanic now knew too many details of my life. I was anxious enough at the thought of meeting Phoenix Carter, now I'd be all sweaty and wrinkled when I arrived. I'd gone shopping to be prepared and worn a salmon colored linen skirt suit from Toby Lerner's and a pair of strappy cream-colored Enzo sandals. My hair was pulled on top of my head with just a few locs draping my face. My intentions weren't to flirt with the young man, but he was still a man and I had to look good. I'd learned long ago that regardless of the feminist movement and women wanting to be equal to men, we still used our sex appeal when necessary to secure an opportunity.

Stepping into the air-conditioned vestibule I took a few minutes to gather myself. I decided to leave my sunglasses on until I sat down. As I approached the table, they both stood up and I couldn't help but notice the way Phoenix looked me over. Mitchell pulled my chair out and seated me across from Phoenix, but close enough to where he had a full view of me. Once seated I surprisingly found myself getting aroused, to the point where I could feel my panties begin to get wet. I mean here he was, a muscular six foot nine inches tall, and about 280 lbs, he definitely had the center of my attention. Phoenix looked very comfortable in his Timberland boots, Guess? Jeans shorts that hung low enough to reveal the waistband of his Polo underwear, a wife beater (a white athletic shirt) and a shiny bald-head to top it off.

But I mostly couldn't help looking at his glittering jewelry. Everything was encased in platinum. His necklace was filled with diamonds (ice as they called it), from which hung a diamond cross. Then there was a large diamond ring; diamond hoop earrings and what had to be a custom made platinum and diamond Rolex watch. He was a walking millionaire, surely the closest I'd ever been to one.

His appearance didn't go unnoticed either. How could it? He seemed to fill up the restaurant with his presence. The manager of the restaurant asked to take a picture with him and there were a few autograph seekers, mostly grown ass businessmen, claiming to want them for their children. Yes, young Phoenix Carter possessed a certain charisma that impressed me.

During lunch Phoenix wasted no time explaining to me what he thought he needed in an assistant, though not really sure of his expectation level. Basically his business affairs, public persona and schedule were a mess and he needed someone, namely me, to organize them. In his words, "his shit was outta order." It was clear that he was of this new breed of athletes who didn't marry White girls, and didn't take well to the rules of the NBA. I told him my background was basically corporate but felt my skills could meet his needs. Then we talked salary, at which time he shocked the hell out of me by offering me $75K with the option to negotiate after the first year. I'd continue to get health and 401k benefits from Mitchell & Ness until we were able to establish Phoenix's business entity. This was almost too much for me at one time. Hell, in addition to having a sexy new boss, I was getting a $20K raise.

With the business side done, Mitchell suggested we talk about our personal lives since we'd be working so close. Phoenix was engaged and had two children. He was originally from Sarasota, Florida but had made his home in Chicago, where he'd been playing since he'd left high school two years ago. He kept a house in Chicago and Florida but also had a brownstone in Brooklyn, for when he just wanted to "chill." I could only guess what that meant. Surprisingly he wasn't the product of a broken home, he had two younger brothers, been raised by both his parents – his mother was a nurse and his father owned a construction company.

I talked about myself and shared with him that I'd grown up with my Dad, my mom having died in childbirth. I told him about my son Owen, who was 21 and lived in LA with his wife and new baby. He couldn't believe I was 38 years old and wanted to know what I did to look so good. The short answer was nothing, my body rarely saw any action since Cole. But I did eat healthy and tried to walk three miles when I could. He complimented me on my locs and told me they were the best he'd seen. Yeah right, I thought, like he hadn't seen Lauryn Hill, shit, he probably knew her. I had to fight the urge to compliment his sculpted arms and long thick fingers. Then Phoenix did what people usually didn't do – he questioned my last name, Borianni. It never seemed to stand out since all Blacks had White folks' last names. With all that said and knowing I had his interest I uncrossed and crossed my long legs in full view for him.

I told him what little I knew about my Italian background, but pointed out that my knack of cooking Italian cuisine proved my heritage. I was startled when Mitchell attested to my skill in the kitchen – I was so lost in Phoenix I forgot he was there. Cooking pasta sauce from scratch came to me as easy as frying chicken, and I definitely made the best lasagna. Even with this, I never acknowledged my Italian side – what was the point? I was a Black woman. So with that Phoenix made me promise that one day I'd fix him an authentic Italian dish.

With Mitchell's coaxing I briefly told Phoenix about the tragedy that had occurred in my life. I told him I'd be keeping a low profile during the civil trial so it shouldn't affect our working relationship. His only question was "Are you still seeing that nigga?" For the first time, I was glad when I honestly answered, "no."

But I missed Cole and hadn't spoken to him since Paulette's suicide, which drove an even bigger stake through the pain and guilt I already felt. Even sitting there being turned on by Phoenix Carter, a young stallion in his own right, my mind never lingered far from Cole. The thought of seeing him again or hearing his voice was probably what kept me going. I knew that no matter what happened that one day he'd reach out to me. If he didn't, then maybe he really hadn't loved me afterall.

Phoenix was eager to get started and offered me a $10K signing bonus, a corporate American Express card and an enormous start-up budget. He immediately pushed me to purchase whatever I needed to get his business organized and running smoothly. I was overwhelmed that a person could move this fast and offer so much money, but I wasn't about to turn it down.

So I accepted and suddenly I was now a personal assistant to an NBA athlete. Hell, the brother was only 23, so how much trouble could he be; I had a son almost that age. But I guess if you add on the fact that he was making $20 million a year, that alone made him a man.

I had to make a few calls – Arshell, Owen and Daddy – to share the news. They were thrilled for me, but a bit concerned about how many game tickets they could get. Arshell however, knowing my history with men, laid down the law when she said, "Sasha, listen to me," I knew she was about to mother me. "You cannot fuck anyone in or around the NBA. I don't care how hot and wet you get, even if it's running down your legs, take a towel and wipe it up. Just don't make that mistake." I promised I wouldn't and assured her I just wanted to make some money. After my past history, the last thing I wanted was a man. Moreso, I was eager to move past the memories of Paulette and Cole. What Arshell didn't know, however, and what I didn't tell her, was that I had the distant question of what it'd be like to get with Phoenix.

Two weeks later I began setting up an office in each of Phoenix's properties and one in my home in Philly. His fiancée and I also met. She was young, 19, with two little boys, ages 2 and 6 months. Crystal was gorgeous, petite, brown-skinned with long wavy hair and had hopes of going to college after the kids started school. They appeared to have a solid relationship, and had been together since high school, so I didn't understand why he hadn't married her yet. Crystal wasted no time telling me that she was quite aware of the many women that floated in and out of Phoenix's life. I wasn't sure if she was telling me this for my benefit or for hers. She did though reassure me that at no time would she ask me to divulge anything that I'd seen or heard Phoenix do. For that I was glad.

At first I had no idea what I was supposed to do as his personal assistant. So I just played it like a secretary and followed his lead. But he kept telling people, "talk to her, she's my assistant." And so it began – people asking me if they could schedule interviews and if Phoenix would consider endorsing their products or events. It seemed the more celebrity you gained, the less money you spent – that's what Phoenix liked. He was also teaching me the same. But Phoenix also wanted me to be aggressive and go after deals that interested him. He didn't just want his own sneaker or a Sprite commercial. He wanted the big deals from Microsoft to Mercedes with a few investments thrown in for good measure. It was clear that my days of sitting in an office answering phones was over.

Mitchell set up his corporation, Carter Enterprises, based in Chicago and initially I was the lone employee. Phoenix's goal was to make money outside of basketball by learning the world of finance. As he so simply put it, "he wanted to learn about anything that had to do with his money."

Over the next month my life turned into a circus. Since Phoenix didn't have an agent, Mitchell reviewed all his contracts. Now, he wanted me to be the first point of contact for anyone trying to get to him. To establish myself, I decided that the best way to let people know I worked for Phoenix Carter was to be seen. Mitchell, in turn, began to tell people that if they wanted any piece of Phoenix, they had to talk to me.

In addition there was the entertainment piece, MTV and BET interviews, record label events, and music videos where rappers wanted his cameo appearance. I attended all these events at his side. Soon my name quickly became attached to Phoenix Carter. I was enjoying it all, meeting celebrities that I'd only seen on television, never letting on that I was impressed by anyone.

I was truly in the fast lane. Phoenix promised me though that once the season started, things would slow down but that for now he had to have his last bit of fun. His entourage typically included his bodyguard, three friends and of course, me wedged somewhere in between. And there were women, Black, White, Puerto Rican, young, old, and they were *everywhere.* Sometimes he'd be with more than one woman in a night. I didn't know where he got the stamina. But it wasn't my job to question his endurance – I only noticed the goings-on and kept my mouth shut.

The first time he offered me a perk, was while we were shopping in Beverly Hills after a two-day commercial shoot with Nike. We'd spent most of that time between a luxury trailer and a tattoo studio where the commercial was being shot. We'd gone to Barney's and then onto Rodeo Drive. It was ridiculous, the ease with which he spent money on himself and others. I saw him sizing me up as he started looking at women's clothes. I protested at first, but he insisted so I let him purchase me a Gucci briefcase, and a pair of Manolo Blahnik shoes. It was impossible to deny him.

At night in my hotel room I would often called Arshell, who never failed to caution me about separating my business and personal life with Phoenix. But what she didn't fully realize was that since Cole, I'd had no personal life.

CHAPTER 4

THE TRIAL

NOVEMBER 1998

By late November I was back in Philly for the trial. Even though Joel tried to prepare me I didn't know what to really expect, but I did know I was scared. Daddy came to court when he could, but, since he felt they didn't have a strong case, he expected me to be alright on my own. Everyone else in the courtroom seemed connected to someone except me. It was like a high school dance, with boys on one side and girls on the other, but this time it was Cole's family on one side and Paulette's on the other.

The hardest part about it all was having to face Cole. They'd even brought his son into court the day I testified. I nearly broke down on the stand, knowing I'd played a part in that boy loosing his mother. I certainly knew what that was like and now I was carrying the guilt of his loss too.

Cole refused to look at me and treated me like a stranger. Even though my lawyer suggested I do the same, I could feel him – feel his presence but I could also feel how he'd detached himself from me. But it didn't stop my heart from aching for him; an ache I knew would never disappear.

Cole's family ignored me. These were the same people – his brother Amir – who we'd often double dated with and his sister whom I'd met, that thought I was, "so good for him." Now it was obvious that I was no good to anyone. And why did Paulette's attorney have to keep fucking pointing at me? I didn't want her to die, hell, I didn't even want her to get hurt. But now even Cole looked at me as if it were my fault, as if *I'd* pulled the damn trigger.

It was hard not to show emotion, as my attorney had instructed me, not to let them know how much I was hurting and how much guilt I really felt. Thank God there were no jurors to stare at me. Just the judge, the lawyers, the families and the empty chair where Paulette would've sat.

I wondered about Paulette. In my five years with Cole we'd rarely talked about her. Our relationship had never been based on his dissatisfaction with his wife. So in order to learn more about her I found myself reading the newspapers that ran a few stories during the trial. According to articles in the *Philadelphia Tribune* and *Philadelphia Inquirer* Paulette had been a devout Christian, wife and mother. Her friends and family said they'd never even suspected there were problems in the Allen household. "I want to give him what he's been wanting over the last five years," she'd been quoted telling one of her church sisters, who naturally assumed it was another child.

Her minister weaved a story of how she worshipped her husband and son. The only indication of trouble was her cousin testifying that she'd asked him to record phone calls between me and Cole. Of course there were never any comments from Cole but the one thing that surprised me was that Paulette and I shared the same birthday, November 3rd.

My mind drifted in and out of the trial. I only half-ass listened as Rankins, Stiles and the medical examiner testified. I could hear their blanket statements. "It was established that Sasha Borianni and Cole Allen had been involved in an affair for about five years. According to police reports, Paulette Allen committed suicide, about 10:00 pm in the bedroom of her husbands mistress, while they lay in bed. At approximately 10:15 pm police responded to a call from a frantic Ms. Borianni that someone had been shot in her home where police found Ms. Allen shot through the head."

I didn't want to turn into some drunk, but I couldn't help drinking myself to sleep at night. During the day I took Xanax, and just to keep my sanity, I sipped Courvoisier on ice or Heineken in between. I had to do something to stop the way my body still ached for Cole. This kept me comfortably numb so I didn't care what people said about me, or how they tried to look deep into my soul to see the part of me that was so cruel, so evil, that I could drive a person to suicide. But no matter how hard they stared, they wouldn't find that dark corner because I wasn't that person. I loved Cole and never wanted to hurt Paulette, much less cause her death.

I thought I was prepared for whatever fate dealt me. I refused to let Joel bring in any character witnesses. It wasn't like I could deny my relationship with Cole. The prosecutor scrutinized every aspect of my life. There was the chance that I would have to pay monetary damages – possibly even give up my house. They had to show by "a preponderance of the evidence" that Cole and I were liable for Paulette's death. I tried to understand what was happening, but it was all so confusing. What did they want from me? All the legal mumble-jumble was driving me crazy.

Joel's services were very expensive, even though he wasn't billing me at the normal rate. When I tried to make payment arrangements with him, he told me my bill had been taken care of by Mr. Carter. Although I questioned Phoenix's motives, I thanked him as he acted like it was no big deal. But I was grateful, because the money Phoenix contributed, allowed me top quality legal advice, which led to a verdict of not guilty. Cole was also found not guilty, but lost custody of his son to his mother-in-law.

Even though we were found not guilty, I knew deep in my heart that we were. Had it not been for our relationship – for me – Paulette would still be alive. The papers had a field day with the story. Mitchell had even been approached with the idea of a movie, which I was totally against. For months I'd kept quiet and avoided the press, but one day I exploded outside the Criminal Justice Center. Unfortunately my quote, which was repeated over and over on just about every channel, was "you can kiss my ass."

CHAPTER 5

CAUGHT UP
December 1999

At first I had been uneasy working so closely with Phoenix but by now a year has passed and it all seemed a blur. I put every effort into making Phoenix, and by association myself, a success. He had stuck by me through the trial and I felt I owed him, and the only way I knew to repay him was through hard work. Over the last year our personal and business lives had become entwined. Although I didn't do anything to stop the changes in our relationship it had began to bother me that the more time we spent together, the more I found myself attracted to him in ways that I was sure weren't healthy. I was grateful at first that he was becoming dependent on me until I began to notice his subtle flirting.

Working as his assistant was more than the executive secretary job I'd envisioned. My job was to effectively manage his activities off the court. I dealt with his public relations, marketing and worked with the NBA league office to make sure everything in his life flowed smoothly. His image was very important to his endorsers and it was my job to leverage these relationships and ensure there were no conflicts of interest. Endorsing Nike shoes and apparel meant it was the only sporting attire he was allowed to wear and it was often my job to lay those clothes out when he made appearances.

We'd spent many hours flying first class and there were times when I couldn't shut Phoenix up for talking about his dreams and the things he wanted to achieve. I was beginning to learn that his tough exterior was just a facade.

I now understood why celebrities had entourages. It was to deal with the loneliness. It really was lonely at the top. I also knew that the reason Phoenix kept so many people around him wasn't because he was worried about getting robbed, it was more so because he didn't want any of the women he ran with to be able to accuse him of rape. He always had an eyewitness lurking. Sometimes his bodyguard would even confront these women and ask them if they knew why they were there. So it would never be any doubt that Phoenix took advantage of them.

During that year the loneliness was also there for me so much that it gripped me with physical pain. When Phoenix would be out with his crew I'd often have my meals in hotel rooms or in restaurants with people wondering why I was alone. I walked the streets in strange cities to pass the time but we were never in one place long enough for me to familiarize myself with it. Phoenix though picked up on this and invited me deeper into his world, probably because I was still dwelling in the lost world of me and Cole.

But I could tell that Phoenix's world wasn't going to be the safe haven I was seeking. It was too fast and there was too much to learn. The hardest part was learning not to accept Phoenix's world as my own.

Having had another increase in my salary, I began to redecorate my house. Since my house was closed up most of the time because of my travel schedule, it seemed Cole's scent, mixed with the smell of Paulette's blood, still permeated throughout. At first I thought I'd needed that scent, I needed to be reminded of the pain

I'd caused, so I co-existed with the lingering odor of death. Eventually, with Phoenix's encouragement, I decided I needed to move forward. First thing I did was add fresh paint and wallpaper, then I carpeted throughout. I bought new furniture for my bedroom and living room, but I still wasn't able to sleep in my bed. I even changed my style of dress. Working in the law firm I'd mostly worn suits and dresses, but now that I worked for Phoenix, I was strictly casual. So as a treat I invited Arshell and her daughter on a shopping spree at King of Prussia Mall at my expense.

I had always been a simple woman. I liked designer clothes, but nothing that shouted a designer's name. Calvin Klein and Ellen Tracy were my favorites, when I could afford it and I usually carried a Coach bag. But Phoenix pushed me to be more daring. Once, while we were shopping in South Beach, he made me buy a pair of tight-ass Helmet Lang pants priced at $450, where he also added a Movado watch. He even tried to coerce me into getting a tattoo. But that I refused. I had to admit I was beginning to like this new lifestyle and all that it had to offer. So when I wasn't bold enough to spend Phoenix type money, he'd just buy it for me, telling me I deserved it. I just hoped he'd get me the pair of four-karat diamond earrings I'd seen. But I could only imagine what I'd have to do to get that.

Working with Phoenix I felt like I was creating an empire in just one person. It gave me a great feeling of power and he seemed unable to resist having me at his beck and call. And he played into my hands by acting helpless without me. He thought I was the strong one but really we were playing off each other's strength.

But we had our disagreements too. The most interesting and political side of basketball was the NBA draft. Earlier in the year I had accompanied Phoenix and Crystal to the draft because he had to do a series of interviews and commentary on the incoming class of players. Their ages ran from barely 18 to 23 years old. When returning from the draft in Charlotte I made the mistake of mentioning to him that I thought draft day reminded me of the slave auction block.

"What the hell are you talking about Sasha?"

"Look at it like this Phoenix. These brothers wait in the "green room" for their names to be called, hopefully in the first round, if they've had the luck of being invited and their prayer is to go to the best team, in the best market for endorsement and most importantly the highest bidder. Then their name is called and they don the hat of the winning team, kiss their family and friends goodbye, hug their more than likely Jewish agent and walk up on the podium AKA auction block to say hello, smile, and shake hands with the head master better known as the "commissioner". From then on Phoenix you belong to them and they can ship you anywhere the want.

"Get the fuck outta here Sasha! Don't nobody own me or tell me what to do?"

Even Crystal chimed in, "So Phoenix you don't think you could be traded?"

"Fuck no, my team needs me. Shit I am the team!"

I could tell my comparison was bothering him but I was on a roll and wanted to prove my point. What the hell did he know anyway?

"Phoenix if your "owner," "Mr. I ain't a slave," thought there was somebody better than you, you'd be uprooted and couldn't really say a word."

"Ain't no way they'd do that shit, not to Phoenix Carter. Anyway you think I care as much money as I'm getting?"

"Yea you care or otherwise we wouldn't be having this conversation. You and I both know there is no loyalty in professional sports. And let's not even talk about the role these shoe companies play, okay?"

"Check this shit out, if these pilgrims wanna give me millions to run up and down that hardwood then I'm taking it. Shit they ain't nothing but a bunch of control freaks anyway. What else they gonna do with that money?"

"Ok, so then let's just say that some of us are getting our reparations." I answered.

We cut the conversation short because I could tell by the number of drinks we were ordering and the stares from the other first class passengers that the conversation had more truth than any of us were willing to admit. But the more I thought about it the more I realized just how entwined politics, sports and entertainment were. Yea, I was learning a lot but so was Phoenix Carter.

Right after Christmas Chicago had three consecutive home games so I decided to visit Phoenix and get some work done. He'd sent his bodyguard, Trey, to O'Hare airport for me. Trey must have weighed over 300 pounds and stood about 6'5" tall. My first night in town, Phoenix, his entourage, and a few teammates, along with me had dinner at Charlie Trotters. You never had to order when you were dining with Phoenix because he usually ordered damn near everything on the menu and just passed it around. He was in a good mood, as they'd just beat Philly by 10 points, which broke their three game losing streak. Phoenix was celebrating with plenty of Kristel. Being with them was always easy and I actually had a good time laughing and talking about the crazy world they lived in and the one I slipped in and out of.

When I was visiting Chicago for more than one night I always stayed at Phoenix's home. Since Phoenix and Trey had been drinking, I chauffeured us back to the house in his Range Rover.

His home was an estate in the prominent community of Deerfield, Illinois, located on the outskirts of Chicago.

Arriving at the black wrought iron gates that surrounded his property, I noticed the property looked dark, with the exception of the soft lightning, surrounding his house, that came on automatically at dusk. I asked him where Crystal and the children were and he responded that they were attending a funeral in Atlanta. Crystal rarely missed a home game as she not only wanted to support him but also kept a watchful eye. I wondered, though, how much of an eye she really kept since Phoenix always did whatever he wanted.

We entered the house through the six-car garage where he kept his two Range Rovers, Ferrari, Bentley and Benz. Once inside Trey went to the guesthouse that was attached by an enclosed walkway to the main house and I went to put my bags away in one of the bedrooms upstairs.

Phoenix decided he wanted to soak in the Jacuzzi, which was situated in the pool house. He suggested I keep him company, which usually meant my sitting in a chair and updating him on his schedule and the various requests for his appearance that poured in. I hadn't drunk much during dinner, so I decided to indulge and poured us a snifter of Hennessy, "Hen-Dog," as Phoenix called it. He started the water for the Jacuzzi, turned his stereo on with Jay-Z singing *Big Pimpin'* and tuned the large flat screen television to SportsCenter. He then took a quick shower and returned with a large white cotton Polo towel wrapped around him.

I'd seen Phoenix naked before so it wasn't a big deal when he pulled the towel off and stepped into the water. I'd always looked at him like the young man he was, even though this time I had to stop myself from looking a little longer at his long, lean and muscular body. The one thing Phoenix was truly faithful to was his rigorous workout schedule. Three times a week, for 2-1/2 hours a day, in addition to practice, during which time he wasn't to be interrupted. And his body showed it, any woman who watched basketball knew Phoenix had the best arms in the league. It was clearly evident that his body alone was enough to seduce any woman, especially me.

Stretching out on the chaise lounge I tried not to look at him, but couldn't help but notice from the corner of my eye that his long dick was quite hard as he slid into the water. While he concentrated on getting the temperature right, I took a moment to steal a look at him, and wondered what it would be like. Once his body was covered with bubbles I felt safe to look his way and begin our conversation.

I began telling him how American Express and Pepsi were seeking his endorsement. I was also keeping score for him on his placement on the All-Star Team. I told him that his summer schedule was slowly beginning to build and he suggested I talk to Crystal to confirm when they would be going on vacation. He also had a commercial shoot with Nike that was set for next week while he was playing in Portland. I continued on about two magazines that were offering to do cover stories on him but I could tell by the look on his face and the way he was pulling on his dick under the water, that he was totally disinterested in my business talk.

Instead of answering my questions, he just sipped on his drink and watched me, like he wanted me. And then just as casually as we were talking, he invited me to get in the Jacuzzi with him. I'd ignored his subtle passes before, but now he was making it very obvious. I pretended to be shocked but somehow during dinner when his leg had rubbed against mine and stayed there, I knew it had been no accident.

Phoenix knew I wasn't seeing anyone and he made sure if I did, that it wasn't anybody he knew. Months ago, when one of the Nike executives had started asking about me, Phoenix rudely told him that I was off limits. I acted as if he was just trying to protect me, but when I told Arshell, she warned me to be careful because it sounded like he was saving me for himself.

I didn't respond as Phoenix continued to ask me to join him. Then as I watched him dipping in and out of the steamy water, I began to feel tempted. In an effort to pull my thoughts together, I stood up and walked over to the floor-to-ceiling windows that overlooked the grounds, trying to reason with myself that it wasn't even right for me to be considering this. I tried to concentrate on the snow that had been falling hard since I'd arrived in Chicago, but standing there looking through the frosted window I felt my insides heating up so I poured myself another drink. It didn't help that Phoenix kept accusing me of being scared of him. I crossed the room and stood against the wall, looking at him. It was clear that he was baiting me. He made it look so damn tempting as he slid in and out of the water, bubbles all over his head. Even with all his millions and his body decorated with tattoos, he was still a kid taking a bubble bath. But this kid was asking a woman old enough to be his mother to join him. By now though he wasn't asking with words, he was taunting me with his eyes.

"Ok, I'll get in, but I'm not getting naked," I said even though I knew it sounded stupid. Laughing, he watched me with those sleepy eyes of his and told me to bring him the bottle of "Hen-Dog." Standing close to where he sat, he looked up at me as I slid out of my tights and stepped out of my wool skirt. I pulled my sweater over my head slowly, 'cause I could see my undressing was turning him on. I stepped into the hot water, wearing a pair of white low-rider bikinis and matching bra, hardly believing what I was doing. While I sat at one corner and him at the other we both broke out in laughter because it was funny. It had to be; otherwise I couldn't have done it. To try to contain my nervousness, I poured myself a full snifter of Hennessy and drank it straight down. My insides were on fire not only from the Hennessy, but because it had been so long since I'd been with a man.

Phoenix, on the other hand, had a lot of women, young, firm bodies that mine couldn't match. I'd seen him with women that looked like they walked off the pages of a magazine and girls that were bred for music videos. Even though I knew my body wasn't lacking, I was still embarrassed for him to see me naked. He didn't seem to mind, and wasted no time in wrapping his long hard legs around my thighs and pulling at my bra straps. I didn't resist so he just unhooked it and tossed it across the marble tiled floor. My breasts weren't big, but they were still full and firm and at seeing them he licked his lips. "Damn Sasha, your shit look good."

I began to accept the fact that there was no way out of this. I just had to be a woman and deal with it. So I said nothing as he eased my panties down and let them float in the water. That's when I felt myself really want him. That's also when he didn't look like a boy anymore. Rather than look at him, I closed my eyes and enjoyed the sensation of his tongue gently licking my nipples, one at a time, until both were hard enough to burst. "See it's not that bad. I promise you're gonna like it," he said, with words that slid from his lips. Then came the kiss. His tongue felt so good moving into the grooves of my mouth, that I gave into him. I knew I was crossing a line from which I could never return but at the same time, I couldn't stop. As my mind swirled with thoughts of resistance and from the hot liquor that was coursing through my body, I felt all resistance slip away.

I was finally able to catch my breath and began giving him a million reasons why we shouldn't be doing this, all of which he had an answer for. He ignored me and in one swift move he sat me on top of him and pushed himself inside me with a force that made me gasp. We both just stared at each other without saying anything while our bodies began to slowly move until I stopped because it was too much for me. But he wouldn't let go; he pressed his lips against mine with a passion I hadn't felt since Cole. Phoenix pulled himself from inside me, stood up and led me out of the water. I was completely in his spell.

He situated me on the chaise lounge, in a position where he could easily enter me. But before he did that, he stretched my legs apart, straddling them on top of his shoulders and then knelt down in front of me and tasted the juices that I'd been holding in since I'd felt this situation unfolding. I tried to reason with myself, maybe justify what was happening but the way he was enjoying the taste of me, all I could say was, "Oh shit!"

The next thing I knew, he was standing up and pulling me towards him. We kissed again and this time he gently pushed my head towards his hard dick, which was standing at attention. There was no protest from me as I moved down between his legs and took him in my mouth. At this point I realized that his dick was as long and hard as the rest of him.

As I tasted a trickle of cum seeping from him, he withdrew from me. I looked up and saw him pull a condom from underneath the chaise lounge I'd been sitting in earlier. Had he planned this, I wondered? Impossible, because there was no way he could've known I would give into him. I tried to hesitate but he pushed me back onto the chaise and plunged himself inside me. I could hear the thumping beat of DMX shouting into my head, *"What these bitches want from a nigga?"* Nothing, nothing – I wanted nothing but what he was giving me right now – while Phoenix pounded the walls inside me. My head was spinning as I tried to push him further and further inside. This time, when we looked into each other's eyes, there was no laughter. We moved and we stroked and I felt myself caught between a dream and reality. I couldn't believe that after a year of knowing him, this boy, more than 15 years my junior, my employer no less, that I had given myself to him so easily…but before I could finish my thoughts…he uttered my name and burst inside me.

CHAPTER 6

ALL-STAR
FEBRUARY 2000

Nothing noticeably changed between us after that. We worked together as if we had never been together. As if he'd never been inside me or like I'd never tasted him. I couldn't talk about it anyway because that would've made it too much of a reality. I think maybe it was as taboo for him as it was for me – that is, until it happened again.

Of course, the only person I could tell was Arshell, who cursed me out after I admitted crossing that sacred line. She begged me not to do it again because she knew the end result would be a disaster. Even with all that said, she wanted all the details. Arshell could easily go from acting like a mother to being a raunchy girlfriend. Even though Arshell lost her virginity before me, I felt I was more experienced because of my entrance into the world of intimacy.

Our friendship had begun in high school after I'd found myself hurting over the first woman I looked up to. There had been an assistant teacher in my English class, Maria. She was a 22-year-old Italian girl who seemed to take an interest in me as I spent time with her on special projects. I immediately took to her and we became friends. One Saturday I ran into her while shopping at Wanamaker's on 13th and Market Streets. She offered to buy me lunch and took me to Kelly's Seafood. We mostly talked about school, with her trying to convince me to attend college after graduation. Before long the conversation turned to boys. She was very eager to listen to all my teenage stories.

After lunch she asked me if I'd like to meet her the following Saturday. I agreed and she gave me her phone number and address. Without her having to tell me, I knew our new friendship was a secret from my friends at school.

The next Saturday I called her and we met on South Street where we did some shopping and she offered to fix me lunch at her house. Her little row home was nice but I could tell she had more money then she made as a teacher's assistant. I helped her prepare lunch where she made salad and reheated left-over lasagna. She was surprised that I knew what ingredients she used and I told her about my having some Italian blood. Maria then wanted to know about my mother but I wasn't comfortable enough to talk about that yet. After lunch we sat on her back porch smoking a joint where I became eager to hear about her boyfriend, Nicki, who was also Italian and owned a pizza restaurant that sold more than pizza. Per Maria, Nicki also sold women, at a very high price, whom he kept housed in apartments around Rittenhouse Square.

The more wine I drank, the more questions I asked about sex that I hadn't asked anyone. I wanted to know why my friends always said it hurt yet claimed it felt good. Then there was the issue of what was the purpose of the clitoris. She answered my questions and in turn wanted to know how far I'd actually gone with a boy. I confessed to having done no more than giving my current boyfriend a hand job until he came. She laughed at this, as she couldn't believe I hadn't yet performed oral sex. I told her that Black girls didn't do that. I also told her I hadn't gone all the way because my father hadn't yet allowed me to get on any type of birth control.

Maria then excused herself to go to the bathroom. When she returned I'd gone into the living room to pour more wine. She came into the room and as she passed by she looked at me and said, "Sasha, you know you can always learn how to satisfy a man, but first you have to learn to satisfy yourself."

Now, I'd never been a timid girl but I was a little nervous. I certainly had never masturbated. I was well aware that touching myself in certain places made me shiver but I always stopped before it felt too good. She must've seen that I was curious, so she asked me if I wanted her to show me. I nodded my head yes. Maria laughed and said, "Don't be so nervous." How could I not; hell, I was sixteen and about to be seduced by a grown woman. Then she moved to stand so close to me that I felt her breasts touch mine. I'd never been this close to another woman and definitely never this close to a White person. She didn't kiss me, just reached for my glass of wine, took a sip and then held it to my lips. I drained it.

Maria gently tilted my head, kissing me on the neck. No boy had ever done that and I felt myself want her to hurry up and teach me everything she knew. But Maria wanted to move slowly. Once she saw that I had placed my hand on one of her breasts she smiled and softly told me how good she was going to make me feel. I wanted that feeling. With that she brushed her lips against mine and kissed me without opening her mouth then moved away. She laughed and held my chin kissing me deep and slow, far better than I'd ever been kissed by a boy.

When she stopped kissing me I felt dizzy from either her kiss or the wine. I stumbled somewhat off balance and she asked me if I was okay. I nodded yes. She then suggested we sit down and led me to the couch. Sitting there with my hands tucked under my thighs I watched her undress. "Sasha, have you ever seen a woman naked?" And with that, she pulled her tight fitting sundress over her head, exposing her panties and bra.

"Not really." I answered while staring at her. Maria had a body like the women I saw on television including breasts that bulged out of her bra and a little ass, which was barely covered with what she called a g-string.

I was wearing shorts and a tube top, which she easily removed. When she was finished I found myself naked in front of her and no part of me was embarrassed. And then she said, "Everything I do to you I want you to tell me how it feels." She pulled me to her and kissed me again but this time she had one hand on my ass and the other on my breasts gently gliding her hands over me. Then she moved her mouth to my neck and bit all around it. I jumped at the feeling and told her it tickled. "Good," she said.

Next she took both my breasts in her hands and told me that a man should always treat your breasts with care and thus she began fondling, licking my nipples and squeezing them just enough to give me pleasure. I couldn't believe I could feel this good and still be a virgin afterwards. My breathing was heavy but I was no longer nervous. "Take my bra off Sasha," she said. I pulled the straps down, turned her around and unsnapped it. Then she turned and told me to take off her g-string. I pulled it down, she stepped out of it and I noticed she barely had hair covering her, where I had an entire Afro. She saw my surprise and told me she'd also teach me how to shave. Now that we were both naked, she took me by the hand and led me to the couch.

Kneeling in front of me she placed her hands on my knees and pulled my legs apart. "Remember," she said, "tell me what feels good." At this she eased her head between my legs and entered me with her tongue. My first reaction was to scream, so I covered my mouth and responded by arching my back, thereby giving her more of me. Maria's tongue roamed the parts of me that were supposed to be private. I was unable to talk until she pulled her head away and told me, "You're not talking to me Sasha."

"Okay," I managed to murmur but couldn't imagine that words existed for the sensations her tongue was providing. When she again planted herself inside me I was half off the couch and began talking to her as I gyrated my pelvis against her mouth.

"Maria, that feels so good." She started to slow down until I begged her, "Please, please don't stop."

She pulled her head away and asked, "Now who else has made you feel like this Sasha?"

"Nobody, Maria, nobody but you."

With that she stuck her finger inside me and took my clitoris between her lips. I screamed out, as I felt a rush through my entire body and a thick liquid oozing from me. After lingering between my legs she stood up and said, "Now see Sasha, you just had your first orgasm and you're still a virgin."

Over the course of the school year my relationship with Maria flourished and I began to trust and look up to her. Each time I visited she made sure a river flowed from me. But never once would she let me do more than suck her breasts because as she reminded me, I was not a lesbian. She just seemed to get so much pleasure from pleasing me. Never once did I feel guilty and I damn sure didn't share my experience with anyone. Maria made sure I'd return each week by providing me with gifts. There was lingerie from stores I'd never heard of, clothes from boutiques, expensive pocketbooks and make-up which was to enhance my beauty, she told me. But mostly I liked the things she told me about how to satisfy a man. There were other things like teaching me to shop at the Reading Terminal and cook like a real Italian where she awakened my taste buds with various cheeses, spices, garlic, and multi-color peppers and onions. I enjoyed it all while Maria teased me, "Sasha maybe you're more Italian than you care to admit."

But our friendship didn't last long because Nicki didn't like my being around and one Saturday while visiting I overheard Maria, in tears trying to explain our relationship to him. When he began slapping her – I screamed to call the police. Then Maria cruelly told me to get out and it was at that moment that I knew that I wouldn't be seeing her anymore.

It was Arshell who found me crying in a darkened classroom and listened to my admission of shame. For what would be the first time of many, she reassured me that it wasn't my fault. Rather than accuse me of being a lesbian, Arshell told me that Maria was just someone I was supposed to meet. But she also surprised me by wanting to know the details of exactly what I'd done with Maria. Thus began my friendship with Arshell and her living vicariously through me. How could I have known that I would continue to provide enough excitement for the both of us?

By now I'd proven myself to be invaluable to Phoenix, as my life existed around his. A cell phone and PDA made me accessible to him 24 hours a day and that's how he liked it. He no longer needed his memory, as he relied on me to know what he needed and to be prepared for wherever he had to go, whether it be professional or personal. The only thing that made it easier was that during the season – November to June – his distractions were few, as all his time was devoted to basketball. I rarely traveled with the team except when he had appearances in respective cities.

I had begun to gather information on setting up his charitable foundation and already had donors. Along with Mitchell we'd been interviewing for a director of his organization. I actually wanted to assume that position, but Phoenix didn't want me in an office, he wanted me around him as much as possible. Phoenix insisted that he participate in ten charity events a year that didn't include any publicity. He'd also begun to hire employees for Carter Enterprises, which had now grown to 70 employees. Their primary business was managing Phoenix's assets and endorsements.

Since I'd come on board, his public image had begun to blossom and in addition to his lucrative sneaker deal, he was the first young NBA athlete to get an endorsement with Mercedes Benz, for their new line of two-seater drop tops. There was also the possibility of him endorsing Timberland, a deal I'd gone after, and practically sealed, without him even being present. Even though people still thought he was an arrogant thug, they couldn't ignore him because he was the leagues leading scorer and the NBA's most sought after player.

Then one morning when I was leaving to fly to Chicago my phone rang, it was the Wilke Lexus dealer of Ardmore, wanting to know if I would be available to accept the delivery of my new truck. I told the salesman I knew nothing about a delivery. However, he informed me that Phoenix Carter had ordered me a new 2000 Lexus, which would be arriving at my door shortly – when the doorbell rang I walked outside and there in my driveway sat a pearl-colored Lexus LX 450 with chocolate brown Coach leather interior. Maybe sleeping with him had been worth it, hell, a new truck with no payments, what could be wrong with that? Now we were both getting perks. When I called to thank Phoenix he laughed and said, "Yo, that's the shit you should be driving, working for me, not no damn Honda Accord."

By February, the NBA was about to break for All-Star weekend with Chicago in their last game against New York at the Garden. I was in the media room, jockeying reporters who wanted exclusive post game interviews. From the television monitor I could see Chicago would clearly win, which meant Phoenix would be in a good mood. Ever since Phoenix had been voted onto the All-Star team I couldn't keep up with the many requests that had poured in and tonight was no different. I had even been considering hiring my own assistant. I'd squeezed in as many interviews as possible and waited for him, along with his boys and Trey after the game. We were flying out the next afternoon to San Antonio for the All-

Star Game, where he'd meet Crystal, the kids and his parents. I'd also invited my son Owen and his wife Deirdre.

Once he finished at the Garden, we had dinner at Moomba and then went to his brownstone in Brooklyn. Knowing I'd be up late making changes to his itinerary, I showered, put on sweats and settled into his office to rework his schedule. I needed to have a minute-by-minute itinerary for Nike, the NBA, Crystal and Trey. I'd learned in this business that nothing was ever confirmed until it actually happened; yet you had to be prepared for anything. But by now Phoenix was no longer tardy for appointments and actually kept the majority of them. Every minute of his time had to be accounted for. It was a big undertaking as he needed to be accounted for during periods when he really would be unavailable. Experience had taught me that Phoenix would be spending that time with another woman, or simply locked up in a hotel room gambling. Knowing him, his posse and his All-Star teammates, they had private parties planned everynight. Thank God I didn't have to be involved in setting those up. One thing I did know was that Phoenix was good for buying and using condoms.

Phoenix had decided not to go out this evening and was upstairs watching a tape of the game he'd just played. Everyone else was out for the night. About 2:00 a.m., just as I was wrapping up, Phoenix came into the office and asked me if I wanted to watch a movie.

We went into his viewing room and began watching *Dead Presidents*, for the umpteenth time. I enjoyed being with him like this, when he was in his boxers and tee shirt, it made me want to treat him like a little boy and take care of him, especially when he complained about his aching body. So when he asked me if I would give him a massage, before I could think about it, I found myself agreeing. He could see in my eyes though that I was questioning what we were about to do next. So, before I could change my mind, he led me by the hand from the couch.

Once in the gym we didn't even talk. I went to the cabinet and retrieved the oils his trainer used, as he quickly undressed. I felt myself wanting to stop what I was doing but a greater part of me couldn't resist. So I went to his stretched out body, oiled my hands with the vanilla and sandalwood blend and pressed my palms into his back. Before long I found myself without thoughts, as I enjoyed the total surrender of him. It was clear from the low moaning he made when I touched a part of him that was more tender than others that he was enjoying it. From his back, to his chest, his body was so surprising, the smooth and roughness of it, with hard muscles that shaped his arms and thighs, which I couldn't seem to massage hard enough.

I could feel the knots releasing in his muscles through my hands. The spasms were passing out of him and probably into me as I worried that even without having sex we were getting too close. It wasn't just my hands; I poured all of me into relaxing him. I wanted him to feel me under his skin. So I continued with soothing strokes, working his entire body, relieving muscle tension and loosening his sore joints. Phoenix's tensions weren't just in his muscles, but were buried deep in his soul far below the surface of his skin.

He tried to talk to me, but the house was too quiet for voices because for once there was no television or loud rap music playing, so I shushed him. But I'd also noticed, as my hands traveled across his slightly hairy chest, that I'd massaged him into a hardness that looked painful. The moment was too good to waste and Phoenix, recognizing this, whined to me like the little boy he was. "C'mon Sasha, please let me put this in you," but I wouldn't stop and instead I began to kiss the places that I'd massaged. Reaching his hardness, I took him in my mouth and allowed him to roam the warmth under and around my tongue. As his body moved closer to the edge of the table, I realized Phoenix was no longer in control and I loved it. Loved him holding on to my head, begging me not to stop – when I didn't he let himself go and his life sperm filled my mouth until his body weakly collapsed on the table. I just rested my head on his stomach until I heard his breathing slow down and knew he was asleep.

Hours later arriving in San Antonio I became panic stricken at the thought of having to see Crystal. I mean this wasn't like it had been with Paulette. I knew Crystal, her family, her children and what was worse is that I'd listened to her cries of Phoenix and the other women she'd found out about. How could I face her knowing I was one of those very women she despised? Maybe it wasn't too late, maybe I could still back out of this affair with her man – too young to even be a man – who moved me in all the wrong ways. Who was I fooling…we were just getting started.

The frenzy of All-Star weekend left me with little free time. The weekend was filled with limo rides from venue to venue. I was being pulled in so many directions I didn't have time to dwell on the awkwardness I felt being around Crystal. My son and his wife were on their own and didn't seem to mind as I'd made sure they had tickets to all the events, having only to make a choice. That's how it was All-Star weekend. Money could buy anything, private ticket sales at astronomical prices, betting, gambling and prostitution were part of the foundation. It was a challenge just getting in and out of the hotel lobby. Fans, athletes, entertainers and reporters covered the city of San Antonio. It didn't help that I was pre-menstrual fighting with a headache and cramps. I had made such a name for myself working for Phoenix that I was even approached by other athletes with job opportunities. I knew though that Phoenix was too selfish for me to entertain the idea of taking on additional work. I also attracted the interest of other men. One evening I'd actually gone out to dinner with a very prominent agent, a White man, who made it known his interest in Black women, and me in particular. Later that night, while sharing a Cognac with him in an intimate corner of the hotel lobby, I noticed Phoenix and his entourage walking towards the elevators. He played it cool but couldn't resist coming over to us to ask, "Yo, what's up?"

Later, after having gone to my room it was only a short time before Phoenix knocked on the door. He pretended to tease me but all the while reminded me that I had a reputation to uphold while working for him. It became apparent what he'd really come for, reassurance that I was still for his enjoyment alone. Luckily for me my period was on, but he could've cared less. So after he begged and pleaded I agreed to go down on him. He couldn't have been more pleased and neither could I, especially when two weeks later he gave me a diamond and platinum tennis bracelet, "for all your hard ass work" he said. The diamonds weren't as big as the one in Crystal's bracelet, but they were still bigger than what I would've been able to afford. He wanted me to wear it everyday, but I only wore it on special occasions like the Essence Awards that I attended with Crystal and Arshell, and the ESPYs that we attended with Phoenix's entourage. To add more credit to his name the East won the All-Star Game and Phoenix was voted MVP.

CHAPTER 7

GOLDEN BOY
JULY 2000

Basketball season was finally over. Chicago had made it to the semi-finals but fell short of beating Philly by 3 points, which made me secretly happy. During the off-season Phoenix usually took vacation during July and then in August and September he began to do celebrity appearances, basketball camps and commercial shoots. I was glad for the chance to get away from the madness of our personal and business relationship, even though for the most part, I thought I juggled it well. I justified it by telling myself that what I was doing wasn't so wrong. I mean I'd done it before but I somehow convinced myself that this time it wasn't the same because I wasn't in love with Phoenix.

July 4th weekend Arshell and her husband were having their yearly barbeque, which I never missed. I drove down two days early just so I could spend time with my best friend before everybody arrived.

Arshell had a beautiful single home situated in Burtonsville, Maryland. She no longer worked full time as a pharmacist but stayed at home raising her three children and going to school for yet another degree. Her husband Wayne R. Wayne (why his parents named him that beats the hell outta me) was a computer analyst at IBM. He was always after me to meet one of his co-workers, but promised that he'd have no blind dates for me this weekend. I often envied Arshell and her happy family life. I knew it wasn't in the plans for me. Maybe before Cole there might've been a chance for me to meet a nice guy but all that died along with Paulette.

The day before the 'que, the house was in a frenzy, so I took the children to the pool. Arshell had a 15-year-old daughter and a set of three-year-old twin boys. When we returned to the house, while the kids were upstairs changing, I sat in the kitchen drinking water and eating grapes, with no thought of who was about to enter my life. Then, in the back door comes this brother about 6'3" tall, golden brown, muscular and fine, claiming to be a friend of Wayne R Wayne. Impossible!

"Well you must be a new friend, 'cause I never met you before." I said as he walked in.

"Actually, I'm an old friend. You are?" He asked, almost sarcastically.

"Oh, my name is Sasha." I answered.

"From the sound of your name I've never heard of you either." He replied, while lifting a case of sodas onto the kitchen counter, all the while taking in my long legs.

"And your name is?" I inquired, looking at the muscles in his back contracting.

"Trent. Well, Ms. Sasha, from the looks of that body, maybe you could help me with these bags."

I began helping him put groceries away. But before we could engage in any further conversation Arshell and Wayne came in the house.

The next day Trent and I still hadn't had a chance to talk because the house was full of people. The men wanted to talk basketball with me and women were competing for his attention. I always found it interesting that I seemed to be a magnet to unavailable men and wondered what about me said I was available.

Eventually Trent caught my eye and he nodded his head for me to meet him in the house. I excused myself and went inside. "Let's take a walk," he suggested. I couldn't have been happier to agree. I did most of the talking; I was probably trying to impress him as we walked behind the development and onto a bike trail. Trent had a way of asking me questions without talking much about himself. I could tell he was a quiet man and it was something about that quietness that attracted me. He never asked me about my past or present relationships nor did I ask him. So from the tone of our conversation I assumed that Wayne R. Wayne hadn't planned this encounter.

I told him my plans for the following week. I was driving back to Philly the next day and from there I was flying to LA to spend a week with my son and his family. Afterwards, I was flying back into BWI to watch Arshell's children for four days while they went on a long weekend get-away. With all that said, Trent thoughtfully offered to drive me home to Philly so I could leave my truck at Arshell's.

The following evening after spending the morning putting Arshell and Wayne's house back in order, we hit I-95 for Philly in his black '99 Ford Expedition. We didn't talk much, just listened to the various CDs he had but he was able to make me laugh – I mean deep hearty laughs and I wasn't even sure what I was laughing about. He wasn't at all impressed by my job and for that I was grateful; football was his favorite sport with the Giants being at the head of that list. We teased each other and made bets, Eagles vs. Giants for the upcoming season. Trent was a 38-year-old electrician for a private utility company and resided in Short Hills, New Jersey. He'd never married, but did have a 13-year-old daughter. He was very knowledgeable about politics and hoped to run for an office one day, the first one being president of the local union. Trent easily told stories about his job, which I found fascinating. Early in his career he'd had a lot of close calls with being electrocuted. Now though, his role was local union representative, in addition to teaching classes at Seton Hall, his alma mater, where he'd majored in political science. Currently he sat on the board of the Joint Apprentice Training Committee and was a member of the Electrical Code Examination Board. He'd been recognized on numerous occasions for outstanding work and was aligning himself with the right people to be ready when election time came. But he always kept his hands in the "heat" as he called it. The only heat I was feeling, was what was rising between us, that neither of us mentioned.

Two hours later when we arrived at my home in Chestnut Hill, it was only natural for me to invite him inside, something I hadn't done with a man since Cole. But Trent, who I'd only known two days, I wanted close to me.

Once in the house I offered him something to drink before he got back on the road. As he stood in the dining room admiring my Annie Lee and EN Brown artwork, I opened him a bottle of Heineken. Watching him from the kitchen, I found myself staring at the very distinct birthmark on the side of his right eye, which gave the appearance of three brown teardrops. I took in his ruggedness and the way his legs held up his body under his AND 1 shorts and sleeveless tee, with biceps that darkened around the outline of his muscles. Trent was a man's man. Even though he was a stranger to me, I knew I wanted him. I wondered, though, if I could have him and we still remain strangers.

Reaching for the bottle of Heineken, I noticed his fingertips were burnished a dark brown, almost black, probably from overheated electrical wires. I had an urge to kiss the tip of each one, but even more so, I wondered what those fingers would feel like inside me. The way he held onto the bottle and looked me up and down I wondered if he could tell how bad I wanted him to touch me.

Before I could focus my thoughts, he moved in closer to me and without asking, as if he knew what I needed, he pressed his lips to mine with a soft, slow kiss that felt like butter melting on warm bread. My shoulders went limp and I was sure he could feel my body give into him in just that instant. When he tried to pull away and attempt to say he was sorry, I only pulled him closer. Then with his lips still slightly touching mine he asked, "You need this, don't you?" I couldn't answer and instead led him upstairs to my long empty bedroom – a room I'd closed off since bits of Paulette and Cole had been left there.

Without invitation, he started unbuttoning my cotton shirt. I tried to talk to him, so I could somehow hold onto the little control I had of the situation but his eyes told me to be quiet. Sitting there on the side of my bed he started massaging my fingertips and then he had both my hands in his – without hesitating I lay back on the bed as he placed his warm hands on my breasts. His eyes were boring deep into me, challenging me not to look at him. I kept closing my eyes – embarrassed that he was pulling me under. But every time I opened them, he was still staring. By the time his hands reached my waist he'd taken his clothes off and seeing his golden brown body I wanted him to take me and asked him to do so but all he said was, "Relax Sasha."

I still had on my skirt but instead of removing it he ran his hands up my thighs and slid my panties down. I laid back on the bed but he wasn't finished yet. Then pulling my skirt down over my feet he began to kiss them. I almost wanted him to stop, the way he was caressing my soles, it reminded me too much of Cole. It was probably wrong but I closed my eyes and imagined he was Cole. Maybe that's why I couldn't hide tears that rolled down my face. And Trent noticed and covered my body with is, brushing my locs back, telling me he loved me. I was so confused as to what I was feeling. There were flashbacks of Paulette standing in my doorway, our eyes locked into each other. A look I knew I'd never forget. Then there was Cole and his black silhouette hovering around my room whispering that he loved me. I wanted to tell Trent to get up from me and run from this room of ghosts, but his hands felt too good. The hands of a stranger were trying to erase my past. Handling me as if I were fragile, something I was so very afraid to be, because I really did want to shatter into tiny pieces for him.

Then there were thoughts of Phoenix and how I had yet started down another path of deceit and destruction. Why couldn't I control myself, my passion, my greed? But then Trent began to kiss my breasts while caressing his thighs against mine. He was so good. There were no sounds, except for the whirring of the ceiling fan and his hands moving against my skin. My body was so warm from his touch, maybe his hands really did hold heat. He was taking me to another space and that's when he began to talk.

"Sasha you're a beautiful woman, you just need to slow down and relax. Take your time. You can't have it all. Baby you gotta let things go – don't hold on forever." I was fading away to wherever Trent was taking me and before I knew it I was crying – not hard sobs but weeping and Trent knew this because I tried to speak but he wouldn't let me. He just laid his body on top of mine, straddling me as he began to massage my head. In between my locs I could feel his fingers on my scalp and he told me not to worry that he would take care of me. And it soothed me yet at the same time I was more than ready for him to take me. "Are you sure?" he asked. "Yes please."

The next morning I was still surprised to see his long golden body lying in my bed. When the alarm went off he groggily woke up looking for me. He found me in the bathroom doing a quick brush of my teeth and washing my face, hoping to slip back into bed with him.

"What's so funny?" I asked, looking at the broad smile on his face.

"Well, Ms. Sasha, I hope you have a toothbrush for me."

I went to pull one out of the medicine cabinet just when he closed the bathroom door, palmed my ass with both hands, and suggested we take a shower together.

While Trent brushed his teeth, I ran the shower and then we climbed in. It seemed all he wanted to do was savor every inch of my body. And I let him. Let him use his hands to wash me with honey and peppermint shower gel. I could barely stand up, so to break his spell I started squirting him with gel and jumped out. He followed me into the room and it was then that I took him in my mouth, and listened to him moan until I could feel his dick pulsating as he exploded inside me.

We lay there exhausted, me sleeping on top of him until my limo arrived and we both had to return to our lives; me to LA and Trent to New Jersey.

CHAPTER 8

BABYSITTER

AUGUST 2000

I was so happy to see Owen. Little O, who was now 2-years-old, had come to the airport with his Dad. He seemed to know who I was because we'd sent many pictures back and forth and tried to spend at least a total of one month together during the year. One of the benefits of working for Phoenix was free travel, which meant I could always see Owen when I was in Los Angeles or as a side trip when I was on the West Coast.

Owen looked good. He reminded me so much of his father. Tall, slim and cocoa brown with strong jaw lines. I'd married his father when I was 19 and it had lasted a good 10 years, that is until he decided he wanted someone with a younger body and more impressionable mind. Thus, he jumped ship and moved to LA with his new woman, leaving me behind with Owen. Even at the age of eight my son became my protector and took over as man of our house. Then about five years ago, when his father had been struck with prostate cancer, Owen moved to LA.

My son was now a schoolteacher in Compton in the winter and during the summer he managed a community center. Deirdre, his wife, was a nurse's assistant at Cedars Sinai Hospital. Owen's young wife was also from Compton; she was petite, jet black and had a real ghetto-girl attitude. Deirdre and I hadn't hit it off at first because I thought she was moving a little too fast, getting pregnant and married within a year. But she eventually proved herself. Especially when she called to Philly one night crying because she'd caught Owen with another woman. Well, that was definitely one of the traits he'd inherited from his father.

During the week, as Owen and Deirdre worked, I kept Little O at home with me and did day trips. I knew Owen and Deirdre were struggling financially, it wasn't cheap living in LA, so I helped as much as they would let me. I went grocery shopping and packed their cabinets and freezer. I even replenished their toiletries – and of course Little O had to have new clothes. I was just glad that my son didn't complain that I did these things. On my last night he insisted that he and I go to dinner alone so we could talk.

Even from a distance Owen had been such a strong man for me during the trial. But sometimes he was too tough on me and I couldn't handle that because he had a way of making me face the truth about myself. I'd always known he hadn't approved of my relationship with Cole, which had probably been part of the reason he'd stayed in Los Angeles.

That night we went to dinner at The House of Blues. He asked me how things were going with Phoenix and I replied that I was working hard. To my surprise he told me that when Phoenix last played in Los Angeles he'd taken him and Deirdre to dinner. Phoenix had been good to Owen too. When he'd graduated from college last year, he'd brought him a Jeep Cherokee; all Owen had to do was pay the insurance and I took care of that. Phoenix always had a way of making sure all his bases were covered.

As we sat talking, me telling him about meeting Trent, he stopped me in mid sentence and asked, "So how are you really Mom?"

My eyes immediately began to swell with tears. He moved his chair closer to mine.

"Mom, do you still think about what happened?" I couldn't answer because if words came out so would the tears. He put his arm around me.

"Owen, I miss Cole so much. But what I mostly think about is Paulette. I mean sometimes O, I can still smell her blood."

"Mom, I'm so sorry I can't be there with you."

I just shook my head. "But I'm getting better and I think having Trent in my life will help," I answered, as I thought back to how safe it had felt having him in my bed.

"Have you told him about what happened?"

Embarrassed, I shook my head no. "Not yet."

"Well have you heard from Cole?" He asked, hoping that I hadn't.

"No, not at all."

All in all it was a good trip – Owen always had a way of making me feel like one day my life would get better and that I'd get rid of the ghosts that haunted me.

Then on Saturday I flew from LAX to BWI, where to my surprise, Trent picked me up from the airport. I'd talked to him twice while in LA and he'd offered to help me baby-sit Arshell's children. I thought he'd been joking but here he was and damn did he look good. He must've spent the last week in the sun, because his golden color had now turned a deep bronze. I couldn't wait for the opportunity to get next to him.

I thought we'd be going straight to Arshell's, but he had other plans. He drove towards Centennial Park on Route 108 where he told me that we were going on a picnic. Now, I liked Trent, but a picnic wasn't what I was looking forward to doing with him. I'd only talked to Phoenix once while in LA so my plan was to catch up on work while I was at Arshell's. I tried explaining this to Trent and he told me to concentrate on my work, that he just wanted to relax and have lunch before we started babysitting.

The park turned out to be a pleasant surprise as he picked a spot near the lake that was filled with ducks and even a few small rowboats. There were children trying to fly kites without wind and adults riding bikes. And it smelled good; dirt, flowers and the water from the lake stirred the love I'd lost for nature. I couldn't remember the last time I'd been to the park.

Once we were situated I opened my briefcase and pulled out my call sheet. I checked all voicemails, began returning calls and making notes. I watched Trent as I did this, and the more I watched, the more my pace slowed. He had fried chicken wings, a salad and deviled eggs. Oh, he was real good. I acted like I wasn't looking as he fixed my plate and doused my wings with hot sauce. Then he pulled ice cold Verdi's out of his cooler. In the middle of a call with Phoenix's Nike rep, I excused myself, put the phone on mute and asked Trent if he was trying to impress me. He said, "If I was trying to do that, I would've taken you to Short Hills." I wasn't sure what he meant but I was willing to visit his home to find out.

Trent sat close to me while we ate. I told him about my visit with Owen and he was glad I'd had a good time and hoped that he could meet him one day. Then of course he had a story about work. About how he had been teaching a class and while talking about voltage and thinking about me he'd actually said my name. His class fell out in laughter and had been teasing him ever since. He was also excited to tell me that the opportunity for him to run for President of the IBEW might be closer than he thought.

After we finished eating we lay back on the blanket talking about what to do with Arshell's children over the weekend. Trent began nodding off and since I couldn't resist his laying so close to me, I rolled on top of him and began massaging his temples. Before I could get to his shoulders he turned me over and began kissing me. It was hard for both of us to believe this was only our second date.

"I can't believe I missed you." He said, sounding surprised, while nibbling on my earlobe.

"Why not, aren't I missable?" I asked, tracing his birthmark with my thumb.

"More than that, but I mean, I just met you last week."

He looked deep into my eyes and asked, "Sasha? Do you know what that name means?"

I raised my eyebrows in question, as if I didn't know.

He answered, "Sasha means protector of men."

"Are you saying you need me to protect you?" I was hoping he didn't.

"Only if you're gonna hurt me."

"Now that you don't have to worry about." I wondered though if he did, because until now I hadn't been able to protect anyone, not even myself.

The weekend with Trent and the children turned out to be the most fun I'd had in a long time. We spent a lot of time at the pool, went to the movies and he even took the twins, Martin and Malcolm to the DC Zoo one afternoon, while Lisa and I went to Columbia Mall shopping, returning with presents for everybody.

Our evenings after the children went to bed were the best, even though they didn't go to sleep until very late. We'd agreed to sleep in separate rooms, me in Arshell's bed and him in the family room.

One night after the kids were asleep I'd sat in the family room with Trent watching a movie. I'd just washed my hair and Trent had no problem oiling the scalp between each of my locs. His oily hands seeming to replenish all the energy that Phoenix stripped from me. This man was slowly easing me into his love. So there we slept, on the floor of the family room.

The next afternoon the kids cooked lunch for us. Trent lit the grill and they made turkey burgers and french fries. The kids had a planned sleepover that night at their cousins in Silver Spring, so Trent and I had the house to ourselves. He insisted that we light the fireplace in Arshell's bedroom, even though it was 80° outside and we had the central air down to 55. So there we lay, in front of the fireplace drinking shots of Stoli and listening to old Teddy Pendergrass CDs. He taught me how and why I should smoke a cigar and turning him on, I practiced licking it slowly and sucking on its wet tip. We both got so horny and drunk that we fell into deep passionate lovemaking. Somewhere in the middle of it all I found myself telling Trent I loved him. Not that it was the kind of love you built over years but the kind that you felt a person had to offer you and I wanted to offer that to Trent. Seeing how vulnerable I was, he began whispering in my ear, asking for parts of my body that I'd only shared with Cole. I told him he could have all of me.

Trent gently turned me over and after kissing up and down my spine, his tongue circled the cheeks of my ass, until I was dripping with longing for him, he slowly entered me where only Cole's dick had gone. I didn't realize how much I'd missed it until that moment. Trent already knew how to talk to me. He'd proved that the first night at my house.

"Sasha, you feel so good. You need everything I have to give to you." "Please Trent give it to me."

"I'm gonna love you Sasha but only if you let me."

I could only moan in response to his love. I wanted to love Trent back but wasn't sure I knew how.

CHAPTER 9

GHOSTS

SEPTEMBER 2000

I couldn't bring myself to tell Trent about Cole or what had happened for fear of what he'd think of me, and I certainly couldn't tell him about my secret relationship with Phoenix. But he made me feel so safe that sometimes I felt if I told him it would somehow redeem and cleanse me. But in reality I knew he would never understand. It had only been two months, so there was no need to rush things.

Arshell couldn't have been happier that I was seeing Trent. She was constantly telling me, with the influence of Wayne R. Wayne, what a good man Trent was and how I deserved to have someone like him. Did they ever stop to think if Trent deserved a woman like me? Arshell emphasized that if I wanted to get serious with Trent, that not only would I have to stop sleeping with Phoenix but I'd probably have to quit my job.

I never felt the need to prove myself nor did Trent ever question whether I was a good enough woman for him. I just wanted to enjoy him without all the bullshit of my life back in Philly or what was going on in the NBA. I knew that within a month my life would be going into high gear at the start of basketball season. We managed to spend just enough time together so that we didn't get bored with each other. He'd been to my home again and we'd done simple things like go to Border's on Germantown Avenue and have dinner at Jake's in Manayunk. The best part was returning, as a healthier person, to Morris Arboretum, which had helped so much to heal me after the tragedy. Trent had even taught me how to re-wire a lamp and replace electrical outlets. The more time I spent with him, the more I knew that my relationship with Phoenix had to end, because I wanted this man to be a real part of my life.

Trent was always getting on me about not taking him outside of what he called my safety net, so I invited him to a Will Downing concert at the Robin Hood Dell, an amphitheater located in North Philly. Never would I have imagined running into Cole.

During intermission as we were returning through the aisles to our seats, I happened to look up from behind Trent and there he was. All 6'4" and color of night that I remembered. For an instant, I forgot about our tragic past and was about to move towards him, when I noticed the woman seated next to him was actually holding his hand. My instinct was to run to him but seeing the hesitancy in his eyes, we acknowledged each other with a nod.

After reaching our seats I realized we had a direct view of each other. Trent didn't notice the connection as he pulled me close to him, asking me if I was cold because my arms had chill bumps. But how could I have been cold when it was so sticky out, so hot that the simplest movements made you sweat. I told him I was fine, even though he insisted on draping his jacket around me. I couldn't stop looking at the side of Cole's face, the smooth blackness that was now lightly etched with lines.

Listening to Will Downing sing his rendition of *"Hey Girl,"* I strained to hold back tears, *"wondering if something inside of Cole had died as it had inside of me."* I tried to imagine what his life had been like since that night. There'd never been any closure, and, if given the opportunity, I know *"I would've begged him to stay."*

After the concert my eyes searched the crowd and the parking lot for him, but Cole had vanished.

Returning to my house I realized that Trent had asked me more than once if I was okay. Finally, to get him off my back, I told him I wasn't feeling well. But he kept insisting that something was wrong. I looked at Trent and hated him for trying to love a woman who still loved someone else. Laying in bed watching television I needed to push Cole from my thoughts so I reached for Trent to make love. And we did, strong and passionate but it didn't help, and I listened as he told me he loved me, while all I could think about was Cole. Afterwards, he must've noticed the far-away look in my eyes that I'd been trying to hide. He sat up and asked, "Where the hell is your head at?" "I don't know," I whispered, turning my back to him and allowing my thoughts of Cole to consume me. I looked around my room and even though there was carpet and new wallpaper the room still belonged to me and Cole. My mind told me that Trent shouldn't even be there. I wanted him to leave and was glad when I heard his heavy breathing indicating that he was sleep. I knew I wouldn't sleep so I got up and went to the bathroom searching for those same Xanax's that had helped me sleep just three years ago.

Two days later there was a message on my voicemail from Cole. He wanted to talk. I was scared to return the call and didn't have to because late that night he called again. The conversation was very cautious, we asked each other the same questions repeatedly. It was obvious we wanted to meet. I couldn't bear for him to come back into my home so he invited me to a friend's apartment in Bear, Delaware the following evening.

I wanted to call Arshell and ask her advice but I knew she'd advise against it so I told myself that I could handle it. I figured I'd wait and tell her afterwards.

The next day he called and gave me directions, no more, no less. I didn't know if I could handle the pressure of being with Cole but I was willing to try. I had a manicure and pedicure, and went to the hairdresser to have my locs set on rods so they could be curly, the way Cole used to like it. I purchased three new outfits, eventually deciding on a faded denim skirt and sleeveless sweater. If nothing else I wanted Cole to remember us like we were.

I arrived at his friends house at 7:30 in the evening and was too nervous to get out the truck. The entire trip I kept second guessing my decision to see him. Why was I seeing Cole when Trent was in my life – there was no need for me to go backwards. I mean I'd just started sleeping in my bedroom again. But as soon as I saw Cole standing on the balcony smiling at me I relaxed and went to him.

I walked into the apartment, which was clearly a hide-out spot for someone. I was surprised at its sparse furnishings, but I was even more surprised that Cole had cooked. He'd fried flounder, baked macaroni and steamed broccoli, a familiar meal for the two of us. But this was not the Cole I knew. In the five years we'd been together he'd never done anything in my kitchen except eat. I guess he'd become self sufficient since his wife was gone. While he set the table we made small talk about the things we were doing in our lives. When I went to sit down he stepped between the chair and me and without thinking I stepped into him – all of him. All three years – all of it just flooded back together. We stood there with me touching his baldhead; kissing all over his face and just not believing I was this close to him again. But he pulled away from me, told me to slow down, that he wanted to talk. What was there to talk about? I didn't want to talk about how it had been over the last few years. Didn't want to hear how hard it had been on him to lose his son. All of that would hurt too much.

Sitting across from Cole and watching him eat was torture. Every nerve in my body wanted him, but I didn't want to be rejected. And so we began to talk. I found out that he'd been keeping track of me and he wanted to know more about my job with Phoenix. That seemed safe to talk about, so I rambled on until he interrupted and asked, "I hope you aren't fucking that boy, Sasha?" I lowered my head slightly. "Cole, why would you ask me that?" "Cause I know what you're capable of." "Well I'm not," I lied. I knew he didn't believe me.

After dinner I helped him clean up and that's when he began to talk about his son. Having lived with his grandmother for two years, Cole Jr. realized that his father had already lost enough. He'd recently turned 17 and had decided to move back in with Cole until he went off to college. So they were now re-establishing their relationship. He claimed that Cole Jr. had even wanted to know about me, and the reason why I'd been in his life. Cole had also sold his house in North Philly, moved to the Northeast and was surprised that I hadn't moved out of mine. I admitted that the reason I'd never changed my phone number was because I'd always wanted him to be able to reach me. Finally I couldn't take it anymore.

"Cole, why am I here?" I asked, sounding impatient.

He shocked me with his tone. "Why'd you come? Are you surprised that I haven't tried to fuck you yet?"

"No, it's not that it's just…"

"Just what? You think we can just forget about what happened?" He asked, moving towards me. There was something about the way his body had tightened that was scaring me. I slowly stepped backwards but simultaneously he grabbed me, almost violently by the arm. I tried to pull away from him but he squeezed tighter.

"Maybe I should go." I said, as I found myself backed against the stove.

"Why Sasha? I'm about to give you what you came for."

This wasn't the Cole I'd known or was expecting. He'd never been violent but since the suicide of his wife, anything was possible.

"Cole, what the fuck is wrong with you?"

Grabbing a handful of my hair he pulled me to him, opening his mouth to cover my lips with his. He started talking, almost in a whisper.

"Sasha, I needed you. You don't know what it was like." I could feel the tenseness in his body as he held me.

"Cole, please, not like this." I pleaded.

"You know how many times I wanted to call you...how many times I drove past your house?"

His grip around me was so tight I could hardly breathe. I tried to wriggle myself free but he began pulling at the snap on my denim skirt, which popped, unzipped and fell to the floor. Before I could reach for it, Cole dropped to his knees, grabbing and holding onto my hips, through my panties he pressed my pulsating pussy against his face. I closed my eyes and felt my body weaken, as he drained me. I couldn't talk, just screamed out his name. I could barely understand his words as he said my name over and over mixed in with the noise his mouth was making against the warm juices that ran from me.

He picked me up, carried me into the bedroom and spread me onto the bed. He didn't move, didn't say anything, just stared at me. I reached up from the bed, pulled him by the waist and unzipped his pants. He never took the time to take his boxers off, just pulled his dick out of the opening and pushed himself far up inside me. I screamed his name again as he pounded my body with his hardness. But it was scary, this ravenous passion. I found myself begging for him to stop, it was too much for me. But all he did was call my name and tell me he loved me over and over until finally, just when I thought he was slowing down, he let himself come into me.

There was no sleeping, he just wanted to take me, over and over and I wanted him to have me. We must have finally slept, because I awoke to the sound of running water. I called his name and followed the sound of his voice into the bathroom, where he sat in the bathtub filled with a sweet musk scent. I climbed in and he took my toes, one at a time and kissed them. Cole seemed to have missed every inch of me, as I'd missed him. Then he asked, "Tell me how it was for you afterwards." I began to disclose to him how it had been for me after Paulette's death.

Lying in bed on Saturday morning, watching Cole sleeping, rubbing his scruffy, unshaven chin hairs against my face, I was determined for us to be together. I decided to fix breakfast, so I dressed and drove to the store for a few items. I had arrived at Cole's on a Friday evening and since being there I hadn't answered my cell phone or checked my messages. I didn't want anything to interrupt the time we had together. At the moment nothing existed outside of Cole's make believe home. While I was gone I phoned Trent and Phoenix and retrieved my messages. Phoenix, of course, was bitching about not being able to reach me all night. I interrupted his little tirade and reminded him that I did have a personal life. Trent, on the other hand was cool, he just thought I'd probably been tied up working with Phoenix. The other call I made was to Arshell, who was actually more understanding of my meeting Cole than I expected. The only thing she didn't agree with me about was that Cole and I actually had a chance. I dismissed her negativity and told her that I had to go. As far as I was concerned, now that Paulette was gone and three years had passed, nothing could stop us.

When I returned to the apartment, I could hear Cole on the phone with his son. I began cooking a breakfast of turkey sage sausage, home fries and eggs scrambled lightly with cheese, just how he'd liked it. We even had orange juice and fresh coffee. Standing in the kitchen turning the potatoes I could feel Cole watching me. He walked towards me smiling and wrapped his arms around my waist, holding my hands as I flipped the sausage. With his face nuzzled in the crevice of my neck, I felt I could've stayed in Delaware forever. We didn't talk, just stood there cooking together in an embrace that I had never forgotten.

After breakfast we talked non-stop about our changed lives. Because of all the publicity, Cole had changed jobs from a high-school teacher and was now counseling abused children. He said it was very hard to find anyone special in his life because he always found himself searching for a woman made up of Paulette and me. How sad. I, of course, couldn't tell him about my affair with Phoenix but I did tell him about Trent.

To our dismay, Sunday arrived. We'd had yet to talk about our future together as Cole kept changing the subject every time I brought it up. I was beginning to think that maybe he no longer loved me. We decided to go out for brunch because it was becoming clear that our fantasy weekend had to end. So after brunch, watching a movie, and making love in the daylight on the balcony, we laid on the couch, wrapped in each other, carefully broaching the subject of our being back together.

"I know this isn't gonna be easy for us to talk about," Cole said.

"It depends on what you want the outcome to be Cole."

"Sasha, you have to understand the consequences of what our being back together would be mean."

I turned to face him. "It means that we love each other. Right?"

His sadness was evident in his voice. "Sasha, baby, you don't understand." I didn't understand and I wasn't willing to give up that easy.

"Look we could...maybe we could just start out slow. Isn't that what we always wanted, not to have to hide? Cole, I know we can make it work. We could even move away once your son leaves for college." I was begging him.

"Sasha, Sasha, it's not that easy baby."

"What's not easy...what is it Cole, are you scared?"

"Look I love you girl, you know that, but I am afraid. I'm afraid of who might get hurt. Our love is too strong, baby. We love so hard that we forget about everybody around us."

"But there's nobody there anymore. Cole, you just have to want it more than you're afraid of it. I didn't want to hear what he was telling me and tried to break his embrace but he held on.

I continued, "Who cares about anybody around us?" knowing what his answer would be.

He held my face so I was forced to look at him. "Yeah but what about my son?"

My eyes swelled with tears while Cole gently talked to me. "Don't cry Sasha, please don't cry 'cause we can't be together, just be happy that we know what it's really like to love someone. It's just that sometimes because of circumstances two people can't always share that love with each other. Please tell me you understand?"

At some level his words began to penetrate. I couldn't fight Cole anymore, he'd worn me down and I was so tired that my thoughts were late in responding to him, so I gave up.

CHAPTER 10

HAPPY HOLIDAYS
OCTOBER 2000

After my spending the weekend with Cole I couldn't wait to see Trent. It would be the first time I'd gone to his condo in Short Hills. Driving up the turnpike my mind twisted and turned trying to still figure out how I could love Cole.

Trent's two-story condo was located in a gated community surrounded by trees and a man-made lake. His condo reflected his personality and his furnishings made it apparent that he'd spent a lot of time at shopping at Restoration Hardware. He was definitely into art, and surprisingly some of it was his own. There was also an entire room dedicated to his book collection. What was even better was that Trent could cook and had fixed a meal of porterhouse steak, stewed tomatoes and rice. I was impressed.

We decided that we would play house for a week and see how much we really did like each other. It was easy to make myself comfortable in his condo, which had a deck that overlooked the vast pinelands of New Jersey. Trent was very easy to be with as he wasn't demanding or too needy. I realized I had no choice, I had to be with him because he was the only man who would admit to loving me publicly.

I stayed in much of the week except for a trip to the mall. During the day I worked the phone setting up Phoenix's final travel schedule before the season started. I was actually enjoying my time with Trent. He brought me breakfast in bed, and I took great pleasure in packing his lunch every morning.

It was a turn on for me to watch him get dressed in his white hard hat and faded jeans that were just tight enough to see his ass and hug his thighs. The sleeves of his tee shirt were always folded twice as he carried his workbag filled with tools and wires, with his lunch cooler under his arm. He'd kiss me and walk out the door with that swagger that twice made me beg him to turn around and take me again before he went to work. He'd just laugh and call me crazy.

In the evenings I cooked big dinners, stuffed chicken breasts, greens, mashed potatoes – I always wore something sexy, usually just one of his button down dress shirts. One night I surprised him, when after a hot shower I'd turned the dining room into a strip club and danced for him on the table while he stuck dollar bills into my garter. We wound up not eating dinner until midnight.

I didn't know if it was better watching him get ready to go to work or waiting for him to come home. I was enjoying the smell of him when he came home from work. Sweaty and musky, especially when I'd take him before he showered cause sometimes I couldn't wait and wanted that smell all over me. I just didn't like the hours in between his comings and goings that I spent alone. In just one weekend Cole had gotten into my pores. He had taken over my thoughts. I couldn't seem to stop wanting him and had to force myself not to page him because I'd refused to take his home number, "in case of an emergency" he'd said. But the only emergency I could imagine would be…that I wanted him, needed him.

It wasn't easy at the end of the week moving from Cole, to Trent, to Phoenix but I had to because it was what had become of my life and I somehow survived by making sure I didn't become too emotionally attached to one man. Maybe having so much sex was my way of trying to fill some empty emotions. My life was no longer my own as all I did was satisfy three men. Loving though, I thought, only one of them. How could I not love Trent? He wasn't smooth like Cole, or a roughrider like Phoenix, but he was all that a woman could want. I rationalized that I slept with Trent because I was guilty of being with Cole and then slept with Phoenix to further remind myself of my low self-worth and what I really was – a deceitful whore. The idea of sex equaling love was starting not to add up.

On my trip with Phoenix to the mid-west it marked the first time I literally slept with Phoenix and did what he wanted everynight, everyday, no matter how many times. It was during this trip that I told Phoenix about Trent, who seemed genuinely happy for me but could've cared less as long as he got what he wanted. And this time in return he shopped for me, in every city, Dallas, Indianapolis, Portland. I didn't even think about what I was buying, just spending his money and it wasn't just clothes, I bought things for my house and had them shipped and as my private cash bonuses increased, out of guilt probably more than love, I bought Trent a diamond-faced Cartier watch.

The only person I didn't keep secrets from was Arshell. She knew the madness my life had become and often I'd just be quiet and listen to her tell me, without judging, that I couldn't go on fucking both Trent and Phoenix forever. That not dealing with the situation was like spitting in the wind.

Arshell had met Phoenix a few times but we never really had a chance to sit and talk, just the three of us. Phoenix was well aware that Arshell knew all my secrets, especially what I was doing with him. Arshell was the only person Phoenix and I could be comfortable with to talk about our affair. After one of his preseason games at the MCI center in DC the three of us went to dinner at Georgia Brown's.

Arshell and Phoenix talked about sports at length since she was a sports buff. Basketball, football and baseball, she was more knowledgeable than me and I worked in the industry. Phoenix often teased her about being a coach-in-training. While they talked I ordered appetizers and drinks.

Arshell teased him that he was "turning me out" and that pretty soon she might want to get her own young boy. Phoenix told her that he was the one turned out. Then for once Phoenix got serious and told Arshell that being with me was about more than sex. He felt that I was the only woman outside of Crystal that didn't just want him for his money, that I actually wanted to see him make something of himself. I was about to interrupt but he continued.

"Arshell you don't know what Sasha does for me. She takes care of my shit and gives me good head."

"I hate you Phoenix Carter," I chimed in.

"Damn," Arshell said.

"No, I'm serious, she know I love her." He was always saying that and I tried not to hear it.

Laughing, Arshell added, "Well, then maybe I should be getting paid for keeping such a big secret out of the *National Enquirer*; 'NBA Athlete Phoenix Carter is sleeping with his personal assistant, Sasha Borianni.'"

"Yo, what you want Ar?" Phoenix asked, probably ready to buy her, too.

"I don't want anything, just make sure you take care my girl," she stated.

Then turning to look at me he said, "Don't worry, she's always gonna be taken care of. Sasha knows she's down for life. I swear on my children."

Trent certainly wasn't the perfect man, even though at times it seemed so, I guess because I was so imperfect. Since we never had the conversation of whether or not either of us was seeing anyone else, it was only a matter of time before I found out about Paige. After my trip with Phoenix, instead of returning to Philly, Trent convinced me to come to New Jersey.

I was alone at Trent's condo one afternoon after he'd been called out during a storm because of some down electrical wires. While I sat in bed flipping through an *In Style* magazine, the phone rang. I usually didn't answer his phone, but when the answering machine clicked on and I heard a woman's voice cursing him out and asking for me, I picked up the receiver. Paige was stunned at first to hear my voice and then asked my name.

"Ms. Borianni," I stated.

"Well I'm Paige and you're the one Trent's been seeing." She said, all in one breath.

"Are you asking me or telling me?" I asked, fucking with her.

"Look, I think we need to talk."

Feeling confident that I was Trent's woman, I answered. "I can't imagine what we have to talk about."

"For starters, I'm carrying Trent's baby."

On that note I agreed to talk with her. To my surprise she lived in Trent's complex so it was only a matter of minutes before she arrived. Well, Paige was clearly pregnant, almost six months and to top it off she was all that. You know the type, about 5'8", light-skinned, hair bouncing and behaving and probably a size 8 shoe.

Paige wasn't a young girl either, as I'd suspected, she was 35 and worked as a consultant for an architectural firm, that's how she'd met Trent. She strolled into Trent's condo wearing a long sleeve, navy blue, Donna Karan knit dress that made her the sexiest pregnant woman I'd even seen. I noticed she moved around his place with ease as if she were very familiar with it. The way

Paige told it, she and Trent had been dating for two years and he'd given her an engagement ring a year ago. But once she became pregnant, he wasn't sure if he was ready. Then, within the last few weeks, he'd told her about me and even started questioning whether he was really the father of her child. She could tell I was surprised with all she was revealing, which made her tell me even more.

My only question to her was what was the current status of their relationship. She said that Trent wanted to get a paternity test once the baby was born, however they were still sleeping together, as recent as last week. Not wanting her to think she'd fucked me up I told her that I'd do the rest of my talking with Trent.

Closing the door behind Paige I thought about the new twist my life was taking. Even though I was having an affair with Phoenix, I had no idea Trent was this involved with anyone else. The difference though was I hadn't allowed myself to get caught. Somehow, knowing he had Paige, made me feel less guilty about what I was doing. How could I argue that he was doing wrong by me? At this point it was clear that we both hadn't been honest. Just because we said we loved each other didn't mean we were committed. What was this commitment thing about anyway? People were always saying that a woman couldn't do the same things as a man and still be a woman. But why not? Why couldn't a woman have sex with multiple men and just do it because she enjoyed it? There didn't always have to be a story of incest, rape, and abuse. At times I certainly thought I enjoyed it. There was something about the way I could flip-flop between men that simply turned me on.

About one in the morning Trent returned home. I was in bed so when he climbed in and attempted to wrap his body around mine, I casually asked him if he wanted to tell me about Paige, his baby's momma. His body was so close to mine at the time that I could feel his heartbeat begin to race. He didn't say anything for a few minutes and then he went into the same story she'd told me, with the addition that she was sleeping with someone else, that's why he'd questioned the baby being his. He adamantly denied that he was still sleeping with her. I told him I didn't give a fuck who was the father of the baby; I just wanted to know why he hadn't told me he was fucking another bitch, especially since we weren't using condoms. He must've come up with ten different excuses. I almost laughed at him.

After that story, I knew that despite all of Trent's good qualities, he was still a dog ass nigga, like all the other men I knew. Which made me like him even more.

Now that I knew there was another woman in the picture I was determined to make Trent mine. He'd been asking me to spend Christmas with his family in New York, but I'd kept putting him off by saying that I wasn't ready to meet his family yet, but after meeting Paige I changed my mind.   But first I suggested he meet my family. At the end of the week we drove to Philly where we had dinner with Daddy. Trent got a kick out of listening to Daddy brag about how at the age of 16 I'd been a woman and taken care of him. He and Trent had no problem getting along as they sat around talking about my father's women and smoking cigars. I knew my father liked him because he kept asking me if he was finally gonna have another son-in-law.

That weekend Trent and I flew to LA so he could meet Owen, and the four of us had dinner at Spago. Owen was impressed and pulled me to the side to tell me that Trent was a good man and that I'd better not lose him. On the other hand, when talking to Owen alone I found him questioning my relationship with Phoenix. I sensed that he knew because of all the extra things I'd been doing for him and his family but there was no way I could admit it. I was just glad to have the approval of the two most important men in my life, that Trent was the man for me.

During our trip I began to realize that I really did love Trent and he expressed those same feelings. The biggest question was what to do with them. We'd gone sailing one afternoon and there on the deck we talked about Paige and his responsibility. He practically admitted that the baby was his but because of our relationship he wanted to be certain. I reassured him that regardless I would still be there for him. Once we were back on shore Trent went out shopping for some imported cigars and I called Arshell, to talk about how I was feeling. My emotions poured from me as I explained to her my confusion over loving Trent and being scared to share my secrets. The two of us tried to decide the best way to ease Phoenix out of my life but Arshell insisted that there was no easy way, that I'd just have to quit. As far as Cole, she was confident that Trent would understand.

I tested the waters and shared with Trent about how I was tiring of my job with Phoenix. Trent admitted that he didn't like how Phoenix demanded so much of my time and felt that I could service him just as well from my home in Philly and not be so dominated by him. In retrospect, his getting Paige pregnant was a small problem in comparison to the life I was living.

We arrived back in New Jersey two days before Christmas, with me having to fly to DC for a meeting with a potential new endorser. Then it was onto New York for Christmas dinner with Trent's family. I don't know why I was so nervous, maybe because I was also meeting his daughter. I just hoped I didn't have to talk about Phoenix all day. Sometimes when I was out, it was as if just because I worked for Phoenix Carter, that I too was a celebrity. Then of course there could be the question of where me and Trent's future was headed. It wasn't that I didn't want a future with Trent but I was scared to let go of my past.

Trent had grown up in Juniper Hills, New York and was the oldest of two sisters and three brothers. He'd also had the pleasure of being raised by both parents. I knew I could handle his brothers, but sisters, well he'd already warned me that they were a pain in the ass.

Trent wanted to get there early but a surprise call from Paige held us up. She was now ready to make demands. It seemed Paige was asking for money. I was glad he didn't want to talk about it – just said he'd handle it. But from the tone of his conversation I could tell she wanted more than money, she wanted him.

Since Trent's truck was in the shop we drove my Lexus, which by now had been replaced with a black-on-black 2001 model, which I hoped would go unnoticed as I didn't want to appear grandiose. I was careful not to over dress and just wore a simple Calvin Klein pantsuit. I had my locs pulled up in a ponytail, silver hoop earrings and a silver Coach watch I'd gotten from Trent. I consciously wore nothing that I'd received as a gift from Phoenix. I wanted it to be clear that I was Trent's woman.

Trent's parents were really nice even though we didn't have much time to sit and talk, as they were busy preparing dinner. I envied how Trent interacted with his family and how everyone simply enjoyed being together. After dinner while everyone was sitting around eating dessert I found myself sitting between his two sisters. One of them was an underwriter for an insurance company and the other a legal secretary. They didn't ask me about my relationship with Trent but were more interested in Phoenix. They wanted to know exactly what I did for him and definitely about him personally.

As with all women who envied my position, they wanted to know how I could resist a millionaire, who was fine, young and probably a stallion in bed. Phoenix had recently appeared on the cover of *Code* magazine so it was evident what his body looked like. They couldn't imagine my not being attracted to him, regardless of the age difference. So instead of telling them I was totally uninterested, I told them that at first I was excited, but quickly forgot about who he was because he was such a slave driver. They also asked the standard question of why young boys spent so much money on cars and jewelry. It was so funny how people always wanted to know the intimate details of a celebrity's life. They even tried to find out how much I made, but I steered them away from that subject by telling them it wasn't enough for the services I performed.

When it came time to open gifts I knew Trent had gone overboard when I saw the blue Tiffany's box. I just prayed it wasn't a ring. Instead he'd brought me a diamond anklet. I knew it was expensive by the size of the diamonds and also by the reaction of his sisters. I just hoped Trent wasn't trying to compete with Phoenix. My gift to Trent was more practical – I gave him two boxes, one with a humidor he'd been admiring and the other held a pair of Prada boots.

While his sisters were running their mouths I looked up and saw Briana, Trent's daughter, enter the room. Briana was tall like her Dad but probably looked more like her Mother, however, what she did have of her father's was his birthmark, which added to her young beauty. I could tell Trent was proud of her and I was glad that at Arshell's suggestion I'd also brought her a gift, a $100 Gap gift certificate.

Trent made sure Briana and I spent some time alone to get to know each other. We talked about school and boys, but she too was more interested in Phoenix. She had her girlfriend along who wanted to know if she could ever meet him. I surprised them both and called Phoenix on his cell so she could talk to him. Realizing she was Trent's daughter, Phoenix invited her and her girlfriend to spend the weekend at his house in Florida. Briana was ecstatic.

CHAPTER 11

COCONUT GROVE
MARCH 2001

Basketball season was in full swing but Phoenix was on the injured list with a slightly sprained ankle. Chicago was playing New Jersey and I was in New York with him for two days for a series of meetings at the NBA league office. Phoenix was well aware of my relationship with Trent and had wanted to meet him but I kept putting him off always warning him that Trent and I were getting serious and I needed to let our thing go, but he refused. So when I accepted his offer to drive me to Trent's, I could tell he was curious to meet this man who was keeping my attention away from him.

Once we reached Trent's complex and parked, I rang the bell and Trent opened the door with a wide smile and juicy kiss, I'm sure for Phoenix's sake. I could tell out the corner of my eye that Phoenix was checking Trent out. I was happy to show Trent off, standing there almost filling the doorway with his smile and open arms for me. Immediately I kissed him, first on the lips and then on his birthmark, which had become my habit. I introduced them and they shook hands with the normal Black man greeting, with Trent inviting him in. I thought Phoenix would decline but he stepped through the doorway.

I went upstairs to put my bags away, leaving them downstairs but keeping my ears open to their conversation. I could hear

Phoenix questioning him about dumb shit, his CD collection, his job, even me. I knew Trent noticed, I just hoped he didn't know why. My hope that Phoenix would soon be leaving was dashed when he accepted Trent's invitation to stay for dinner. While Trent went into the kitchen I asked Phoenix what he thought he was doing.

"I just wanna get to know the nigga and make sure you alright."

"Shit, I'm 40 years old and can take care myself. What do you know, you ain't but 25."

He slid down into a dining room chair, grabbing his dick, as was his habit when he was trying to make a point. "I know one thing, and that's what we did at my house last night means that you're not that fucking serious about Mr. Trent."

"I hate you Phoenix Carter."   And with that he just gave me that sly grin as Trent re-entered the room.

So there we sat at the table, the three of us having dinner. It wasn't so bad and I had to admit I rather enjoyed it. Phoenix even made it a point to confirm our visit with Briana to his home in Florida. The two of them mostly talked about sports. Phoenix was surprised that Trent hadn't been to one of his games yet. Even more surprising was Trent asking Phoenix how he handled all the pressure of his female groupies. I listened as Phoenix boasted about his lifestyle as if he were really confident with who he was. I knew better. I had seen a side of Phoenix that he tried to hide from everyone, even Crystal. Phoenix was vulnerable and suffered from a bad case of insecurity. He often admitted to me, sometimes in tears, the pressure of being a superstar, of having your private life invaded by the world. People scrutinized every play you made on the court and every move you made off the court; your entire life was open to speculation and opinion.

Phoenix happily rambled on about all the "smuts" he'd been with. Then in a smart-ass move he said to Trent, "Ask Sasha, she knows how women be all over me." And I did know, but I just shook my head in disgust.

Contrary to his often-brash attitude and our twisted relationship I did have a genuine love of basketball and actually loved to watch Phoenix play. His ego was big enough so I never told him how much his on-court performance turned me on. It was just something about when he went to the foul line. His shoulder's tightened, body became slack and he would rock, back on his heels, forward on his toes, with his muscular arms contracting as the ball floated to the net and his hands dropped from the wrists in the follow through.

Looking around the table at our threesome, I realized I had always been good at betraying people. But this time I was weaved in a web of having an affair with two men simultaneously, with Cole still hanging onto the edges of my thoughts. But I knew it wasn't right. Trent didn't deserve to be part of my sick world. The strange thing was that sometimes after I'd been with Phoenix, I wanted Trent even more. Why had I turned out like this? I'd never planned on being a "bad girl." The good girls had always taken my boyfriends when I was young. They were always prettier and smarter and had a mother. But me, I had been raised by a hustling limo driver whose values weren't – and couldn't – be the same as those in a two-parent household.

The following weekend, the four of us, Trent, Briana, her girlfriend and I arrived at Sarasota International. To make it special I'd reserved a limo to pick us up at the airport. I wanted to do my best to not only impress her but to give her a lot to tell her friends back home. Phoenix was due in Chicago on Sunday afternoon so we had to make the best of it.

Pulling up to Phoenix's Coconut Grove estate I was more concerned about what Trent might be thinking. He was aware I worked among money but I wasn't sure if he could deal with it up close and personal. The only thing he made me promise before we left New Jersey was that I wouldn't work over the weekend, and I agreed.

Crystal set us up in the guesthouse, which had four bedrooms and was more like a mini-mansion. The kids had a great time swimming with Trent and Phoenix while Crystal and I barbequed. Phoenix offered to fly us to Disney World on Saturday morning, but the girls preferred to stay at the house. As with his home in Chicago, Phoenix had a fully furnished game room. A pool table, video games, ping-pong and a theater-sized television, where for some reason he was able to view all the current movies.

On Saturday night, Crystal's nanny came over so the four of us could go out. We went to a private club in South Beach for dinner where we met up with Phoenix's celebrity counterparts. Phoenix made sure to impress Trent by introducing him as his, "ole head" rather than as my man. When Phoenix and I found ourselves alone I thanked him for inviting us down and was glad that him and Trent were getting along. He just laughed and told me, "We should, shit we got enough in common."

"The only thing you have in common is me."

"That's about enough ain't it Sasha?" he asked while pouring from one of the bottles of Moet he'd ordered.

"One day, Phoenix, I'm not gonna be fucking your arrogant ass anymore."

"Oh yeah, when's that gonna be?"

Later that night when Trent and I had finished making love, he told me there were a few things we needed to talk about. The first was that it was finally time for him to begin his run for IBEW President for the local union in Paramus, New Jersey, which would mean fundraising, meetings with some Italian Mafia types and a lot of political bullshit. I was happy for him because I knew this was what he'd wanted. That is, I was happy until he gave me the second half of his news. Paige had delivered a baby boy and Trent had been there. I was furious that he'd kept it from me, but the worse part was that he was the father and planned to take an active role. Pissed off that he'd kept it a secret, I chose to sleep downstairs on the couch and almost wished I could've gone to Phoenix.

Laying there on the couch I realized how truly fucked up my life was. Maybe I really wasn't anybody's woman. Here Trent had a daughter, and now a son, that would take up parts of his life where I couldn't even compete, and what did I really have with Phoenix? Maybe I needed to remove myself from both relationships. Maybe I just wasn't good enough to belong to any one man.

There never seemed to be one man solely for me anyway. How long would I continue to envy other women for what seemed to come so easily to them and so hard to me? Why was I always left feeling like a penny waiting for change? I even resented my mother for leaving me. How could she go, how could God take her knowing I'd be so alone? Left alone to understand why men wanted me, and why I always attached myself to the ones that belonged to someone else. My Daddy had cheated on her, I'd read it in her diary, but she'd painfully accepted it as if it were part of marriage because he was good to her. She was the reason I'd moved to Chestnut Hill in the first place, cause she'd written about it, that it was, "a quiet old town that seemed to let you live a slower life compared to West Philly." If only she'd known she was writing to me. Maybe I could've learned some lessons a girl can only get from a mother. As hard as I tried I could never imagine her voice or her touch. I knew she was pretty, we even looked alike. But no matter how much of her diary I read, or the number of pictures I stared into, I still couldn't find the woman who was supposed to be my mother.

With the news of Trent's baby I changed my return flight from New Jersey and flew into Philly. Arriving at home Monday morning I found a note from Robertson's florist who had attempted to make a delivery. I drove around to Germantown Avenue thinking that Trent was trying to make up to me. But I was surprised because instead of the dozen multicolored roses Trent usually sent, I found an arrangement of exotic flowers. And instead of the card being signed "Love, Trent" it read, "Because I'll never stop loving you. It was signed "A Dark Stranger." I knew that it could only be from Cole.

I decided to let Trent spend some time with his new son. Phoenix's schedule was fully focused on basketball because of the playoffs, so I worked from home. I stayed in Philly for three weeks, doing all the things I hadn't done in a long time. I visited Daddy, shopped in Center City, read three books, cooked comfort foods and reacquainted myself with my home. I even took out time to go downtown to Total Serenity for a full day of spa treatment. By the end of the three weeks, Trent was begging me to come to New Jersey and I found myself yearning to see him.

I drove to Short Hills on a rainy Thursday afternoon and decided during the ride that I would begin to accept Trent's son as part of my life. But more importantly I needed to find a way to end it with Phoenix. He must've seen me parking my truck because he was at the door when I walked in. When I entered the condo I could smell he was cooking pasta, but before I could head for the kitchen he stepped into my path and pulling my hands behind me, he handcuffed me.

"C'mon Trent stop playing, I'm tired." I said, tired from my drive and irritated about all the things I'd been forced to think about.

"You should be, you been gone for three damn weeks." He said it as if he didn't know why.

Encumbered by the cuffs, I slowly followed him into the kitchen. "Trent, please take this off I have to pee."

Instead of removing them, he led me into the bathroom where he lifted up my skirt, pulled down my tights and panties and asked me if I needed help sitting down. I sat and peed while he watched but he never cracked a smile. When I was finished he pulled toilet paper from the holder, wiped my ass, front to back, adjusted my clothes and washed his hands.

Now I was pissed. Stumbling into the kitchen, the smell of pasta sauce mixed with garlic and pesto made my stomach growl. Standing next to him as he stirred and tasted the food, I asked. "Trent, can you take this shit off?"

He ignored me. I bitched, frustrated that I couldn't put my hands on my hips.

"Damn, nigga, if you didn't want me here then maybe I should've stayed the fuck in Philly."

"Who the fuck you talking to like that Sasha?" he asked. "What you think I'm one of them fucking thugs you run around with?"

Before I could say another word he spun me around and grabbed me by the cuffs.

"You think you're the one that's running this relationship. That you can just pull away from me without talking about how I feel, huh Sasha, is that what you think?" Holding my arms up, so that it hurt, he threw me against the table, practically bending me in half; he yanked up my long wool skirt.

"Trent what the fuck is wrong with you?" Instead of answering, I could hear him pull up a chair behind me and that's when I felt him tasting me, right through my panties and tights. He was sucking so hard that I could hear my tights tearing. I wanted to turnaround, grab his head and push his face further but his arms were around my waist, pinning me to the table, keeping me from moving.

He stepped away from me and cried, "Sasha, you're fucked up, how could you stay away from me? You know I love you. Paige don't mean shit to me. You hear me?"

"Yes Trent I'm sorry." I heard him open a kitchen drawer. I had no idea what he was doing until I felt him cutting away at my tights and panties. "Oh God," I moaned, realizing I was being seduced not only by Trent but also the smell of my heritage seeping from the stove.

"You better call somebody cause I'm getting ready to fuck the shit outta you."

By now he was on his knees, where he inserted two fingers inside me and teased my swollen clit with his tongue. I couldn't believe he was doing this but I also didn't care. I begged, "Please, please Trent!" I just wanted all of him inside me and begged him to remove the cuffs, still he refused until finally the juices that flowed from me were running down my thighs. Roughly, spreading my legs apart with his knees, he shoved his golden hardness so deep inside me that my knees buckled but he held me up and further spread me out over the kitchen table until he collapsed on top of me.

CHAPTER 12

HAPPY BIRTHDAY
MAY 2001

The more I tried to separate myself from the sordid business and personal relationship Phoenix and I were in, the more I was being sucked in deeper. I never romanticized about what could be. It wasn't like we loved each other and wanted a life together; it was just that I couldn't pull myself away from him.

Phoenix had recently played a playoff game in Philly with a layover of two nights, both of which he decided to spend at my house instead of at the Four Seasons with his team. He didn't want to go out, just lay around for me to wait on him, as if I didn't do enough of that as his assistant. It was times like these, when we were intimate, that I could get him to agree to business ideas that he'd otherwise reject. I was constantly telling him that he had to be open-minded about the opportunities that didn't bring him money but offered exposure. Carter Enterprises had expanded and would soon be offering a clothing line. I'd made him subscribe to the *Wall Street Journal, Fortune* and *Black Enterprise*. He even took my suggestion to get a personal chef, college tutor and media trainer. He would now be able to take advantage of all sound bites and make the most of his television appearances. Phoenix knew how to dress but I hired a personal tailor to help him refine it by making sure he had crisp white monogrammed shirts and even though he had expensive shoes, I forced him to make sure they were always shined, even if he had to do it himself. Phoenix was slowly transforming from a thug, all about money, to a young entrepreneur learning how to make smart investments. His keen business acumen allowed him to manipulate business meetings dressed like a thug but with the mannerisms of a CEO. Yes, Phoenix was growing up.

With Phoenix in town, Daddy came to visit with a woman who surprisingly, seemed to be his age or at least close. I could tell she had money, when they showed up in her Lincoln LS, with her swinging a Chanel bag and some unnamed designer outfit. A little flashy, but that's how he liked them. She was pleasant enough and even knew who Phoenix was, as I watched her paw all over my father.

The atmosphere was just too relaxed for Phoenix to only be my boss and this Daddy immediately picked up on. Daddy's hugging me and whispering in my ear, "I see you taking good care of yourself Sasha," confirmed that there was more to my relationship with Phoenix then just business. But Daddy was cool and didn't do anything to embarrass me. I'd fixed a pot of homemade sauce and linguini, at Phoenix's request, along with a salad and garlic bread. I even had cannoli's for dessert. Daddy didn't say it, but I knew he liked it when I showed off my Italian cooking skills. Along with the wine I'd brought, I'd also made a pitcher of Long Island Ice Tea. The more they drank the more I worried that Phoenix would relax around them too much. Unfortunately, I did overhear Daddy tell Phoenix, "I appreciate you taking care of my daughter." So after they took some pictures and Phoenix signed some autographs, I sent them home.

Being at my house was the first time we really allowed ourselves to show affection, we lay in bed, wrapped around each other – our long legs entwined like a Philly pretzel, eating hot wings and watching movies.

But during those two days he ravished me sexually. Phoenix was able to find every nook and cranny inside my body while my only advice to him was he should slow down and take his time with a woman. The road to the finish line was always more fun than the finish itself.

Before his visit was over, Phoenix had an unusual request, that I have a small vault installed inside my house. I knew he had one in each of his homes, where he kept money, jewelry and a few guns, but I thought it was strange that he was insisting I get one. I told him I had a security system linked to the police station, but that wasn't his reason. Phoenix wanted to hide a few things and me being interested in what they were, agreed. He said it would be a small steel box hidden in the floor of my bedroom closet. In return for my silence he told me I could get a car that would totally belong to me. I immediately chose a silver BMW 735I to go along with my Lexus. His instructions were that every month a package would arrive via Federal Express, and I was to simply put it in the vault.

Now I had been aware, mostly from eavesdropping that Phoenix had been involved with a Chicago jeweler, as were other athletes, who'd been killed while on business in New York. The details were shady but I knew that Phoenix was somehow involved. I just hoped his putting a vault in my house didn't put me at risk. But what was worse is that I hoped the risk would pay off.

Soon after Phoenix left Philly, Crystal called and said she needed to fly into town to speak with me. I wasn't concerned that she knew about me and Phoenix because she hinted that it was about Phoenix's birthday in two weeks. Mitchell had told me in the beginning, "build a solid relationship with Crystal but don't make her your friend." He never warned me though about Phoenix, I guess he thought I'd learned my lesson from Cole and Paulette. I hadn't.

I met Crystal one afternoon for lunch at Rouge on Rittenhouse Square and found her all excited in asking me to assist her in planning a surprise birthday party for Phoenix at their home in Chicago. I couldn't turn her down because she rarely asked anything of me and she was offering $2,500.

I agreed and we made some preliminary plans. It was going to be a surprise party and Crystal was excited that we would have a secret Phoenix knew nothing about, since he always claimed to know everything. My role would be to secure the guests, logistics and the entertainment.

So it went, for the next two weeks, together we planned his party. Spending so much time with her made me feel guilty, especially since I was fucking her man. As the date neared she insisted I meet her in Chicago so we could shop for clothes at her expense. So there we were, in and out of shops on Michigan Avenue buying dresses, shoes, bags and accessories. Watching Crystal I prayed for her continued innocence, that she would never find out about Phoenix and me.

Finally the party day arrived and the people who'd shown up on his behalf did surprise Phoenix. I'd invited Trent but he was wrapped up preparing for a fundraiser to be held the following evening in New Jersey, to which I was to accompany him.

It was a classy party but you always had to remember that this was Phoenix Carter and he was a young boy. His hip-hop friends were there and took care of all the entertainment in addition to inviting some women (video girls mostly) to add to the ambience. Since it was the end of the season and everybody wasn't in the playoffs, a lot of his counterparts were in attendance: KG, Half-Man-Half-Amazing, AI, Starbury and MJ, who I would've much rather been sleeping with. Then of course Mitchell reminded me to invite Phoenix's staff and business partners, which included folks from Nike, Pepsi, Gatorade, Timberland, American Express and Mercedes.

The atmosphere was heated, the music loud and you could find people throughout the house doing everything from dancing to making deals. The food was catered from a mix of Phoenix's favorite restaurants while Cristel and Moet flowed from a fountain all night. There were waitresses, parking valets, and bathroom attendants. I couldn't imagine what gifts people would bring a millionaire, but they brought things that I knew he'd never use or wear, things he'd probably just give away. Looking around at his guests and thinking of all my accomplishments I realized I'd finally made the big league but at the same time I knew my time was running out.

Phoenix treated me like his prized employee during the night. Too often though I found him near me when I was talking to other men, sometimes even abruptly interrupting and always touching me. He never said it, but I knew Phoenix didn't want another man near me. He accepted Trent because he didn't travel in his circle and he enjoyed knowing I had a man waiting for me in New Jersey while he was fucking me at every opportunity.

It was practically 4:00 a.m. when I realized that mostly everyone had left except Phoenix's close friends so I made my way to the guesthouse. Crystal stopped me. "Sasha, can you come with me please?" she tentatively asked.

For a moment I panicked thinking maybe she was about to confront me. Had it shown on my face during the party, maybe Phoenix had spent too much time near me.

"I wanted to give you a little something to say thank you," she said, motioning for me to follow her into their bedroom.

I was nervous and hoped she couldn't tell. "Crystal you paid me, that's enough."

"It's obvious Sasha, you've done more for Phoenix than I can possibly imagine and we wanted to give you something to show our appreciation." At that moment Phoenix walked in the room. My heart was pounding as I awkwardly found myself standing between the two of them, in their bedroom no less. Smiling, Phoenix put his arm around my shoulders and guided me to sit on the bed. I couldn't imagine what the hell they could give me, I just wanted to hurry up and get out from between them.

Crystal then opened her jewelry cabinet and pulled out an unwrapped long narrow blue box, which, surprisingly, held a 22-inch platinum necklace. Before I could find the words to thank her, she pulled out a second box, a smaller one. In it was a platinum and diamond watch pendant to be hung from the necklace. Even though this was typical Phoenix, both were actually classy pieces and not gaudy like some of the jewelry they wore.

I was speechless and although I tried not to, tears fell. Not because of the gift, but more so because of the backstabbing person I was. By now Crystal and Phoenix were standing so close to me I could barely breath. So I stood up, kissed Crystal on the cheek and thanked her, all the while trying not to look at Phoenix. But then he hugged me, which made me almost want to spit on him.

Finally, I made it to the guesthouse where I took a long shower and washed my hair. I was exhausted. There was no way I would continue with Phoenix I told myself. I wouldn't endure another season, no matter what the price.

Once I was in bed I phoned Trent to see how the race was going. He, too, sounded exhausted and made me promise I'd be in Newark airport by noon so we could spend some, "quality lovemaking time" before the fundraiser. I told him about the gift from Crystal and he said I deserved that and more. He didn't think that just because my salary was now $150K that Phoenix appreciated all I did for him. Trent's main complaint was that

Phoenix was too needy of me. So after enjoying a little phone sex, we said goodnight and I drifted off to sleep. I was eager to get home to him.

It had to have been at least 6 a.m. when I heard a light tapping at my door. It could only be Phoenix. "I know you hear me," he said as he turned the knob and entered the room.

I managed to sit up in bed. "What are you doing here?"

"C'mon, I need you tonight, Sasha." He answered, standing at the foot of the bed.

"This is the wrong fucking place to be needing me. Go to your damn wife."

"She ain't my fucking wife yet!" He said smugly. I could tell he was fucked up, he'd been smoking blunts and doing shots of Grand Marnier all night. As he moved closer to the bed, I wrapped the sheet around my naked body.

"Listen, just let me…"

"Let you what Phoenix? Fuck me while Crystal is a few feet away?" I could see him get agitated, his face tightening, reminding me of him on the court when he was desperate for the last shot.

He raised his voice, "What the fuck do you care? You ain't cared about Crystal before!" He said, slurring his words.

"Well I care about her now and you know what Phoenix, it's over and I don't just mean this shit we been doing. I'm quitting!"

He laughed. "Bitch, you ain't going nowhere. You just biting Crystal's ass cause she gave you that platinum and ice." He said nonchalantly, sitting on the bed, unbuckling his belt.

I moved closer to the headboard and threatened to call Trey.

"Trey can't help you – he left with some bitch."

"Well, I'll call Crystal in her room then."

"Yeah and what you gonna tell her? That you been fucking me and tonight you don't wanna give it up?"

He was right. What would I tell her? It was inconceivable to Phoenix that I didn't want to give myself to him. I tried to turn from him but he grabbed me by the throat, forcing my face close to his.

Gagging I said, "Phoenix please – I can't."

"Fuck that, yes the fuck you can!"

I managed to loosen his hands and quickly got up from the bed, attempting to go into the bathroom but he stepped in front of me and held my arms. We tussled as I tried to get out of his grip but even fucked up, he was too strong for me. I fell against the dresser, knocking my toiletries over. He wrestled me to the floor, all the while telling me how good I was to him. Screaming at him I fought to get loose, he slapped me. I tasted blood. "Don't make me do this Sasha, please." In an effort to fight him off I grabbed for his platinum chain scratching him on the neck. He tried to pull my hand loose but I yanked even harder until his chain snapped. That didn't stop him. I cried, "Phoenix please stop, I can't do this anymore."

Then with a sudden quickness he picked me up and threw me on the bed, knocking over a full-length mirror that shattered to the floor.

"You know I need this Sasha, right? I only do it because I love you." He said, pinning me to the bed, his knee across my stomach. I winced from the pain but he wouldn't relent.

With this he removed his pants and boxers all at once, still holding me with one hand, as I lay there limp beneath him. Straddling me, he roughly pushed a finger inside me while whispering in my ear. "Don't you know how fucking bad I wanted you tonight. Why you making me do this shit? Shit, I fucking love your ass. Feel how hard you got my dick." I didn't respond, just laid there crying. He slid down and buried his head between my legs until I could feel my body defy me as my orgasm melted around his tongue. Why was this happening? Why couldn't I control my own body? Then he rose up on his knees, put both my legs across one of his shoulders, and plunging himself deep into me he came.

He knew he'd made me come, so to prove it he pushed his finger in me and then put it to my lips and grinned. I looked in his eyes and wanted to tell him I hated him but knew it wouldn't matter. Finished with me, he picked his broken platinum chain off the floor, stuffed it in his pocket and walked out. I now realized that my affair with Phoenix had sucked the life out of me. He had no remorse.

I was trembling, and at first I just lay there under the covers crying, thinking maybe I really did belong to him. I hated myself for what I had become. Maybe it wasn't the men I hated, but more myself for what I let them do to me. For a moment I even thought about suicide, yet another selfish act. I phoned Arshell and tried through tears to tell her what happened. She couldn't talk with Wayne lying next to her but said we'd talk later because they were driving to New Jersey to attend Trent's fundraiser. So from somewhere I rummaged up the strength to pull myself together. I mean maybe it wasn't that bad – wasn't it just a piece of pussy? I had to leave for the airport in a few hours so I staggered to the shower, got dressed, while being careful not to cut my feet on the broken pieces of glass.

Once I was ready I phoned Trey's room, as he was supposed to be taking me to the airport. He said he'd be up to get my bags. Upon seeing the disarray of my room and the broken glass, he asked me if I was okay. Then reaching for my bag he noticed my swollen lip, which I hoped would disappear before I reached New Jersey. I knew I didn't have to explain. I went to the Benz to wait for him, where he showed up with a plastic bag filled with ice.

Sitting in first class I realized that I'd have to act as if nothing happened when I saw Trent. I longed for one of those nights when

Trent and I would spend the evening together in the same room without talking. Thinking I couldn't do it, I heard the steward ask me what I'd like to drink so I ordered a double shot of Remy Martin. By the time I reached Newark Airport I was half drunk.

I walked off the plane and before I could look for him, Trent's arms consumed me and all I could do was cry. He laughed and thought I just missed him since I hadn't seen him in almost a month. But it was so much more. I was crying because once again I'd fucked up my life and was scared of how all this would end. Would someone die again because of my fucked up choices? Of course this was no time to figure it all out. I just pushed it into the back of my head and told myself it was one of the hazards of the job. So I told Trent I missed him and was glad to be home.

Traveling to his condo, making love was the last thing I wanted to do but I knew I couldn't turn him down. I definitely couldn't let on that anything was wrong. Why did he have to be so damn happy to see me? The swelling in my lip had gone down but when I finally removed my sunglasses Trent questioned my puffy eyes. I played it off that I hadn't slept in two days. That's when he suggested that maybe I needed a real vacation. Poor Trent had no idea what I really needed and neither did I.

Eventually we wound up in bed and I lay there, responding to Trent as if he was all that mattered. I said all the things I knew he wanted to hear. It was the first time I ever faked it with him.

"Oh, Trent, I love you." But did I?

"Trent, it feels so good to be back home." How could it, when my body still ached from Phoenix's violent lovemaking?

"I missed you, oh I missed you so much." I thought about all the men I'd repeated those words to and wondered if I'd ever meant them.

I got through the rest of the afternoon by falling asleep until Trent woke me up to get dressed. While Trent was in the shower I checked the messages on my cell phone. Six calls from Phoenix, begging for forgiveness. What he was really begging for was my silence, as I heard him ask me what it would take to keep me.

As I was pinning my hair up I heard Trent in the living room arguing with someone and I knew it was about the Union. I was stunned by the words coming from him. Trent was threatening to kill somebody. He sounded like a madman. Was everybody going crazy? When I heard the door shut I went downstairs. I asked him what was wrong. "Sasha, stay outta this alright." Even though he didn't want to tell me, I'd heard bits and pieces of the conversation and repeated them to him verbatim. But he just turned, looked at me with a seriousness that made me cringe and walked away. It was now obvious that running for IBEW President wasn't going to be an easy feat for a brother.

I'd convinced Trent to rent a limo for the night so Wayne and Arshell could ride with us. When they arrived at the condo I couldn't even meet Arshell's eyes. The event was being held at the Sheraton in East Rutherford. There would obviously be no time for Arshell and I to talk prior to leaving.

Making our way through the mirrored lobby, I looked at us, the happy couple. Trent was wearing a black double-breasted Versace suit that I'd forced him to buy, having agreed to buy him the black Ferragamo shoes he was wearing. He looked good, how could I not be proud to be his woman? Entering the crowded ballroom I smiled and greeted people as Trent and I walked around the room. I could tell Trent was happy to have me beside him because he couldn't stop telling me how beautiful I was. I'd brought a charcoal-colored Dolce & Gabanna dress that was cut down in the back so deep you could just about see the crack of my ass. With that I wore a pair of black Jimmy Choo heels I'd special ordered through one of Phoenix's contacts. I also displayed the tennis bracelet I'd gotten from Phoenix and a pair of diamond hoops. As good as even I knew I looked, on the inside I felt like I belonged to Phoenix Carter.

To my astonishment, as Trent's campaign manager was reading off the list of donations, I heard her say Phoenix Carter, $5,000, which received a loud applause from the audience, and some people knowing I worked for Phoenix, turned and smiled at me. I couldn't believe him; here he'd forced himself on me earlier that morning and now he was contributing to Trent's campaign, which of course he did to let me know how much power he had.

While Trent was mingling with his guests, Arshell and I went into the lobby to talk. I told her what happened with Phoenix and quickly admitted that it was my fault for having been with him in the first place. I realized I'd always been a dick tease, always wanting some man, any man, regardless of who he belonged to. Arshell felt otherwise. She tried to convince me that Phoenix had raped me; not only physically, but had raped my spirit. I wanted to believe her but told her that until I quit, that it would continue to happen. She was furious.

"Sasha, do you know what rape is? It's not about sex with Phoenix; it's about power and control. You're clinging to a situation that has outlived its usefulness. He's made you compromise all your morals and values." I was trying not to cry as she talked. "I mean, look Sasha, you can be a whore, who gives a fuck? Sometimes I wish I could fuck a few different men, but damn don't let Phoenix control your life. Do you really wanna lose Trent over that nigga?"

Maybe I did. I didn't deserve a man like Trent.

I could barely speak up. "Arshell, I'm bought and paid for. Look at it, ever since Cole..."

"Shut-up with that Cole shit. You can't ruin your life because his crazy ass wife killed herself. How long are you going to blame yourself? What happened Sasha, to the person you used to be? When's the last time you read a book? Lit a candle? Hell, all the plants at your house are dead! Phoenix was never there for you. What he provided was just an illusion."

By then I was crying, at which point Wayne R. Wayne walked up to us. "What's wrong with Sasha?" He asked.

Instead of answering I ran to the ladies room.

It was well past midnight as Trent and I returned in the limo to his condo, then I did something that I only did with Phoenix. I pulled a joint out of my purse and lit it. The sweet smell of it made me begin to relax. We both just sat quietly, passing it back and forth.

"Sasha, we need to start thinking about our future. What do you think about us getting married?" He asked, as he ran his hand down the back of my dress touching my ass.

"Yo, are you serious?" I caught myself, I was starting to sound like Phoenix and his thug friends and it wasn't the first time. I looked at Trent, who hadn't even noticed and passed him the joint.

"Golden Boy, I wouldn't want to marry anybody but you. But now I have something to say."

"What?"

"I'm quitting my job with Phoenix." I stated.

"When? I mean why?" He asked putting the joint out in the ashtray.

"Its just time to move on."

"Is that all there is?"

Did he expect there to be more?

"Yes, and the fact that if I'm going to be your first lady, I need to be closer to my husband."

"Well, you need to be sure that's what you really want, cause you've been real important to Phoenix." Was he saying this because Phoenix had just given him $5,000? Was he now ready to reap some of the benefits of my fucking Phoenix? I didn't answer, just leaned forward and told the driver to take the long route to Short Hills. As he slowed down, I moved to the seat across from Trent and slid my dress up to my thighs.

"Why don't you stop worrying about Phoenix and take care of your wife?"

Since the incident in Chicago, Phoenix repeatedly tried to tell me he was sorry but I kept all our meetings and phone conversations strictly business. I'd even threatened to press charges if he ever tried to touch me again. But he tried to buy me back into his graces with all the things he thought I wanted. All I really wanted was to be free from him. First I declined all his presents; an all expense paid trip to Tahiti for Trent and me; a 500sl Mercedes Benz and in one voicemail he even said he'd leave Crystal. I just declined everything, sent the Benz and the tickets back and never even responded to his talk of leaving Crystal. But I knew I was weakening.

While we sat one morning in a conference room at Sony, waiting to discuss an endorsement deal, without saying anything, he gently slid a box towards me and I could sense what it was. My heart began beating rapidly; his eyes begged me to open it. I lifted the hinge that held it closed, and looked onto the pair of 4-karat diamond earrings that I'd been waiting for since the first time I'd slept with him. These I knew were bigger than Crystal's. I just shook my head and without looking I could feel him relax, realizing that he'd finally won me back. Before I could thank him, the Sony execs walked into the room. Whispering, he patted my thigh under the table, "Yea, now I got my Sasha back."

The affect of my sordid relationship with Phoenix was bringing out an ugly side of me. My emotions were spiraling out of control and lately I was short tempered with Trent and was beginning to avoid him. I wasn't even returning Arshell's phone calls. I knew it was out of hand when I found myself arguing with Phoenix. Instead of us returning to our usual shit he began to play games with me. After the gift he'd just tease me but wouldn't sleep with me. I found myself at times wanting him, craving him. I tried to tell myself that I didn't care; yet when he didn't want me I was disappointed which made me want him even more.

Trent had won the election and wanted to look for an engagement ring but I kept making excuses. Then I found myself getting jealous of Crystal who had by now set a date for their wedding. I mean it was hard to sit by and watch her spend money, making plans for their big day and I couldn't even look Trent in the eye. I'd also discovered that the FedEx packages being delivered to my house were carrying uncut diamonds. I'd been tempted to take one for myself but not knowing who was involved in a scheme this big I changed my mind. Once when Phoenix had asked me to listen to the messages on his cell phone I overheard a few names of who might be involved and was glad I hadn't gotten that greedy. I never commented, just read him back the messages and when he gave me a look that read 'you don't want to ask any questions', I didn't.

One particular night I was in Chicago because Phoenix was in the finals of the playoffs. He didn't know until later that night, when I called his cell phone that I was in town. Before I knew it, he was knocking on my hotel door. After hesitating, I opened the door and there he stood. A six foot nine thug in a gray Sean John sweat suit that hung from his body with the same attitude that he had. Who was I fooling? He entered the room and strolled over to me with a look of ownership. He asked me why I hadn't told him I was in Chicago and why I hadn't come to the game. I tried to explain that I'd arrived late and was tired, especially since we had to be in a meeting with the team owners in the morning. He accused me of lying because Crystal had said she'd talked to me earlier in the day and had asked me to go with her to see her wedding gown. That was it!

"I don't want to hear about Crystal, her fucking Vera Wang dress or none of that bullshit!"

"Oh, so that's why you won't help her with the wedding." Phoenix exclaimed. "Wait a minute – I know you ain't jealous. You kidding, right?"

I screamed at him knowing all of this was leading nowhere. " Fuck no, I ain't jealous, I'm getting married! I'm just tired of fucking with you."

He didn't say anything just sat slouched down in a chair by the bed.

"What do you mean fucking with you? I haven't touched you, Sasha?" He said, sounding condescending, knowing I wanted him.

"Look, Phoenix, you're getting married and I'm engaged to Trent, so please let's stop this bullshit." He began quoting some damn rap song by Philly's Most Wanted "*excuse me chick what's your name – 'coupla dollas ain't it, so wuz your game,*" as if I couldn't understand what it meant. I hated him.

"Sasha." he said calmly, as he reached for me. "I don't care if both of us get married, I'm still gonna fuck you."

Why was I relieved? He was so damn sure of himself as he reached his hand between my legs, grabbing a handful of pussy.

"Look, I know we fucked up doing this shit too much, but its too late now. I'm never letting you go."

I just grabbed him by that platinum cross, pulled his mouth to mine and kissed him. He pulled away and said, "Yeah, right, that's what I thought you wanted."

CHAPTER 13

PROTECTOR OF MEN
JUNE 2001

There were some decisions I had to make, and the only way to clear my head was to visit Arshell. I had been ignoring her for too long and of all the things I'd sacrificed, I wouldn't risk losing her.

I flew from Chicago to BWI to spend the day with my friend. Arshell picked me up and we drove to her house so we could talk. Actually, it was more so I could listen. She put it real simple, resign from my position with Phoenix, get honest with Trent (not about everything) and at the same time she suggested I go into therapy. It seemed Trent had even phoned her to find out why I was being so hesitant about moving forward with our wedding plans. It was the first time I was caught speechless. I could no longer rationalize or justify my actions.

Instead of flying back to Chicago, I reserved a limo and took the long drive home to Philly. To my surprise there was a message from Owen telling me that his wife was expecting. I had to call him and when I did it was hard to share in his happiness and that he picked up on.

"Mom is something wrong?" he asked.

"No, I'm okay." I mumbled.

"Well that means something's wrong. Have you heard from Cole?" He always thought any problems I had were related to Cole. Probably because he knew how much I'd loved him.

"Oh, Owen, I wish it was that simple but nothing in my life is simple, not relationships, not work. I just want...."

"What's wrong with work?"

Then he must've felt it.

"Mom, is something going on with you and Phoenix?" he asked, impatiently.

I couldn't answer him because I didn't want to lie.

"Mom, Mom, please tell me you're not fucking that boy!"

"Owen it's not what you think. It's not the same as Cole. It just happened."

"Mom, nothing just happens with you!"

"O', please just let me explain."

"No Ma – I gotta go." And he hung up.

Owen had never done that before. Even with all the wrong decisions I'd made and warnings he'd given me he'd never just hung up and shut me out of his life. Was I now gonna loose him too? Rather than call back I decided to wait until I had better control of my situation and then I'd go talk to him in person.

I wanted to keep my leaving Phoenix as simple and professional as possible, so I phoned Mitchell and requested a meeting the following day. In his office I didn't hesitate but simply told him the situation, that I'd been sleeping with Phoenix, about the rape, all the gifts and that at this point our relationship was out of control.

He didn't respond at first, just stood up, and walked around his office, staring at me from across the room. He then sat on the couch and motioned for me to sit next to him.

"What happened, Sasha? I mean how did you let it happen? You're supposed to be older, mature. That's why I thought you could handle him."

"Well, I couldn't." I said, determined not to cry.

"So now what do you want to do?" He asked, sounding defeated.

I handed him the resignation letter and after reading it he just shook his head in disbelief.

"You know he's not gonna *let* you quit."

"What do you mean, *let* me?"

"He'll offer you more money. Sasha, he really likes you, and you're so good for him."

"Mitchell, are you asking me to stay, to keep fucking this man?" I got up and paced the room, trying to further enunciate what I was saying with my hands.

"Well, I mean you could stop and just tell him it has to be strictly professional."

"Mitchell, it's too late for that and obviously you don't know your boy very well. Every time he sees me, he wants to fuck. He doesn't care who's around or where we are. He thinks he fucking owns me. And you know what's even more fucked up, is that I'm starting to believe he does. But the difference is I don't wanna be part of his little threesome anymore." I paused. "Mitchell, please talk to him."

"Sasha, who is gonna do your job?" he asked, as if that was my problem.

"I don't know, maybe one of his other women or one of the secretaries at his company would be glad to take my job. Anyway, that's not my problem."

"So what do you want? You know there's going to be some legal ramifications."

I started walking towards the door. "Look, just give him the letter and get back to me."

"When was the last time you spoke to him?" He asked.

"Well, we haven't really talked in about a week. We've just been leaving each other voicemails.

"Alright, let me try to talk to him."

Later that night Mitchell called me on my cell while I was at Trent's. I took the phone into the kitchen.

"Sasha, look it's not good." Mitchell said, sounding like he was afraid to tell me of Phoenix's reaction.

"I'm listening."

"Like I predicted, Phoenix refuses to let you go. He says he'll do whatever you want, more money, a new house, car. He says he can't live without you, that you owe him."

"I owe him! Is he fucking crazy? I made Phoenix fucking Carter the man he is off the court and he says I owe him!"

"He wants you to fly to Chicago and talk to him. Sasha, I mean maybe you should try talking with him. He says that he'll stop having sex with you but he needs you by his side."

"Fuck that Mitchell! I'm not for sale any more!"

"Well I might as well tell you that he says he'll make sure you don't work for any other celebrities. He can blackball you Sasha."

I didn't realize I was screaming. "You know what Mitchell? If Phoenix fucks with me I'll ruin his goddamn career. I'll let Crystal know we've been fucking and if I have to I'll go to the press and tell them all the other corrupt shit that's been going on throughout the league and Carter Enterprises. And do you think I don't know what's in them dam FedEx envelopes Mitchell? You think I'm gonna keep my mouth shut about that if he fucks with me?"

As soon as the words were out my mouth I regretted it because as I turned, there stood Trent who'd heard every word I'd said, especially about me fucking Phoenix. We stood staring at each other. I could hear Mitchell still talking but I wasn't listening. Trent walked away and I told Mitchell, who was in mid-sentence, that I'd have to call him back. I slowly walked into the living room.

"Trent please just listen to me." I pleaded.

"You dirty bitch! I knew there was more to you and him than just fucking work!"

"Please Trent you don't understand."

"Fuck no, get the fuck out!

I went to him. "Please Trent let me at least explain! I…" He didn't let me finish, just unleashed his anger by backhanding me across the face.

I knew then there was no more to be said. Anyway, what could I have said?   Sorry would have meant nothing. Explanations would've been useless, as if I really had any. But somehow I wanted to explain. Wanted to finally tell him about Cole, and about how Phoenix had pulled me into his life and that the sex was only because I'd been weak, been empty. That it was him I really loved. But that would've all been bullshit.

Trent's hardened face warned me not to say anything. So I just picked up my bag from off the recliner, grabbed my pocket book and walked out. As I opened the door I looked back to see if maybe I could say something but he turned his head, reached for the remote and acted as if I'd already gone.

CHAPTER 14

THE NIGHTMARE
JULY 2001

First I was him, and then I was her, but the sex was so strong.

I found myself laying underneath her with all her weight on me, talking to me. The lovemaking was good, long awaited. It was as if she had the dick and was pushing it deeper and deeper inside of me. My body though was rising to meet her and the thrusts she was gyrating against me. Why was it so good? I couldn't stop the thoughts or the act I was webbed in. Didn't she realize who I was? Regardless that it had been years since she'd seen me. Hadn't been around me growing up, didn't know if I'd needed training wheels to ride a bike or if I played with snakes. All we both seemed to know is that we wanted each other.

And then I was her. Giving it to him, making him love it and me. I knew it was good to him. I could tell by the way he cried out "Oh Mommy, I missed you." But he hadn't asked me to stop and I wouldn't have been able to. It wasn't that he looked like his father; it was just that I longed to be his mother, his mommy. He was hurting, and loving him was the only way I knew how to heal that pain.

I woke up sweating with my pussy throbbing as if I had stopped myself short of coming. I had to still be dreaming but, no, the sun was coming through my blinds. I opened my eyes and quickly closed my legs. Damn, why were my thighs wet? My pussy needed me, a finger, a stroke, anything to make the throbbing and yearning go away. But I was scared, so I squeezed my legs tighter and rolled over to figure out what had gone wrong in my mind during the night. Why had I dreamed about a mother and son having sex and why had I been both of them?

After having this nightmare I knew it was time to talk to somebody about what had happened in my life. It was time to go beneath the surface of my false strength and bravery. So at Arshell's suggestion, I made an appointment with a psychologist.

Over the next two weeks while waiting to hear from Mitchell, I focused my attention on finding another job. I realized it would be hard to find a position that would pay $150K, plus expenses, in addition to the perks I received from being with Phoenix. I didn't even know what kind of job I was looking for. But what I did know was that Corporate America would give me something stable, no traveling, just 9-5 and two weeks vacation in the summer. I needed to re-establish myself through honest work that had a purpose.

The position I now found myself in was much different than anything I'd ever dreamed for myself. I mean my idea of a successful career as a young girl was whatever career the latest Barbie doll had accomplished. Whether it be airline stewardess or nurse. Funny though how being an only child I often had to play the part of two Barbie's and even had to play Ken who was forever trapped in the middle having to choose between the two. So was my life.

There were no ideas of what I wanted to be when I grew up, I just grew up. Once I'd graduated high school I'd tried college for a year at Temple but it moved too slow so I got a job at Blue Cross where I met Owen's father. After we married I moved on to become an executive secretary at Wharton and once the marriage was over I began working for Mitchell and Ness, where all my troubles began and somewhere in between all that I was divorced and Cole happened.

Now here I was, starting all over again. I had a professional resume done and registered with a headhunter. Where could I go? Where could I hide? I searched DC, LA, Atlanta, and Boston. Everything seemed boring to me. I couldn't imagine myself returning to the standard secretarial life. Sitting in an office all day taking orders, typing memos, curbing personal calls and scheduling meetings would drive me crazy. And of course there were the one-hour lunches spent with White girls sharing personal stories, who otherwise wouldn't speak to me. I didn't know what I'd do but I couldn't return to that, at least not right away.

My bills were all current and, thanks to Phoenix, my house was paid off. I'd saved $100K in cash, made wise investments in the past few years, so at least I could afford to take some time off. I knew I'd probably walk away with a tidy sum of money.

Walking the streets of Chestnut Hill, up and down Germantown Avenue nothing seemed familiar. My neighbor's faces had even changed. There were new families, mostly young professional couples who knew nothing about Sasha Borianni. I was glad for the strangers, yet missed the familiarity. Even though I tried to absorb myself in the job search, many days and nights I found myself doing what most women do when they're hurting. I'd thrown away any Xanax's I'd had leftover so all I could was drink wine, some nights I'd go through two bottles. WDAS FM once again became a comfort to me, as Luther Vandross' words spelled out my pain reminding me, *"That Hearts Get Broken All The Time"* but what was even more true was that this time *"I'd broken mine and become one of love's casualties."* It's funny how music can hurt you and heal you at the same time. I attempted to turn away from the sound that was sealing my pain but I was curious to find out who the hell this chick Jill Scott was, that everyone in Philly kept playing. Had I really been out of touch that long? It was this sister's words that made me realize that my life was no longer defined by one of Phoenix's rap songs. My relationship with Trent had been a ballad set to her tune of *"Taking a Long Walk"* but because of my selfishness, I was clearly *"swimming upstream"* most likely to the unknown.

Daddy phoned, but I wouldn't take his calls. I assumed Owen had told him what happened. Finally he left a message saying, "Sasha, like I've always told you, life is like a crap game, if you don't win on the first roll, you just shoot the dam dice again. Remember baby, Daddy loves you. Call me alright?"

By the end of June Chicago had won the championship so Phoenix would now be all that he'd imagined himself to be. He just wouldn't have me along for the ride.

Mitchell eventually calmed Phoenix down and proceeded to draw up legal documents, I was due a large severance pay. According to my contract I would be paid for the remainder of the year, in addition to bonus money Phoenix owed me, which totaled $275K. I knew some of that was hush money. Unfortunately, I would have to return the Lexus and BMW. Thank God I'd kept my Honda Accord. I'd hardly driven the cars, they were usually either parked at my house or Trent's. The first stipulation was that I work to train his new assistant and any files at my home were to be turned over to Mitchell. And of course I had to sign a confidentiality agreement and there was to be no publicity. The other stipulation was before Phoenix would sign anything he requested that I meet with him privately.

We agreed to meet at Mitchell's office and for the first time, in a long time, I didn't care what I wore. When I got there Phoenix had already arrived. Mitchell directed me to the conference room and told me to holler if I needed him. I was feeling confident until I walked into the room and saw him spin around in that chair. He rarely wore suits, but today he had on a chocolate brown, Hugo Boss single-breasted linen suit that I'd picked out. Underneath he had on a cream-colored mock turtleneck by Ermenegildo Zegna and a pair of chocolate brown Prada shoes. His baldhead was shining, as were the diamond hoops in both his ears glittering. I wasn't sure if I preferred him as a boy or a man.

He stood up and walked towards me and that's when I realized how truly weak I was. He grabbed me around the shoulders with one arm and quickly kissed me in the mouth, tracing my lips with his tongue. "Yo, what's up Sasha?" He said, as I backed away from him. I didn't answer just took a seat. I expected him to sit across from me or maybe at the head of the conference table but no he sat right next to me, so I could smell him. And I did smell the Angel cologne he was wearing and I felt myself begin to want him. Then he sat back, slouched down in his chair, resting one hand on his Gucci belt and smiled that sly grin at me. Nervously I stood up.

"Look Phoenix, I can't work for you anymore." I stammered.
"Why not?" he asked, not even looking at me.
"You know why not." Hoping I did.
"Maybe I do, maybe I don't, but how 'bout you need to tell me." He said casually, but looking at me intently as if he dared me to find a reason not to want him.
"Look, I can't be your business manager and your 'ho, okay?"

"Damn – who said you was all that?" He asked, while stroking himself, for my benefit I'm sure.

"Phoenix I don't know why we had to meet anyway. It's pretty cut-and-dry, I'm resigning," I said, standing behind the chair I'd been sitting in.

"Do you think you can just up and go, just like that? What about how I feel?" He almost sounded pathetic.

"That's not my problem." I said, as I sat back down, this time further away from him.

"Oh yeah and you might wanna get your damn diamonds out that vault at my house," I added, trying to change the subject.

He looked surprised that I'd opened one of the packages.

"I'll send somebody for it. Look, let me ask you something. You think you gonna be satisfied with that fucking Trent nigga? C'mon, you and I both know you need more than that Sasha."

I ignored him, I wasn't about to tell him that because of him I'd already lost Trent.

"Don't fucking patronize me you bastard!"

He got up and moved towards me. I stood my ground. I thought he would grab me, I almost wanted him to but instead he just stood towering over me. He didn't speak just stared down at me; until I could feel my panties get wet, like they did the first time I met him. To gain some leverage I stood up.

"Alright, fuck it, if that's what you want!" He said, moving close to me.

I shook my head yes and attempted to walk around him but this time he grabbed me from behind, cupped one of my breasts and whispered in my ear, his tongue touching its lobe, "So you don't wanna fuck me anymore?"

Then it clicked, all his power and control over me he was about to lose. So I turned around, grabbed him by the dick and said, "Fuck no!"

CHAPTER 15

SURRENDER
AUGUST 2001

I still hadn't heard from Trent and was scared to call him. Now that he was IBEW president I'd recently seen him on the news, holding his son no less. I wondered if he was with Paige now, if they were a family. I hated the thought of it but knew I had no recourse with all the humiliation I'd caused him. But I was glad that he was doing well and only wished him the best. So later that night as I lay in bed unable to sleep I decided to write him.

Dear Trent:

I pray for your understanding as you read this letter, because I know there is no forgiving me for how I betrayed you. I guess writing you helps me see the real crime I've committed against you and the trust you put in me. Somedays I just can't seem to sort it all out. I know there is no way to justify what I've done to you but there are some things I want to share.

Before I met you I'd been in love with a married man. I stayed in that relationship for five years until one night Cole's wife broke into my house, and as I laid in bed with her husband, she shot herself while standing in my bedroom doorway.

Six months later I was working for Phoenix. Working for him at such a fast pace seemed to fill in the spaces of my life that had previously been filled with ghosts. What I didn't realize was that attaching myself to someone of his stature made me vulnerable, which he took advantage of. What's worse is I let him. I felt worthless, but what did it matter? I'd held myself responsible for Paulette's death, which only compounded the guilt I'd always felt and hid of my mother having died giving birth to me. Now I was responsible for two deaths.

Ever since I was a child I'd hated the sight of blood, maybe because as my father had told me, that giving birth to me, my mother had hemorrhaged so badly that I'd almost drowned in her blood as I was passing through the birth canal. And then there was Paulette's blood. It had soaked through my hardwood floors and it, too, drowned me. Although Owen cleaned it up, it took my very breath away and months later I found myself still trying to scrub away the smell of death. And then one night, unable to sleep, I began rearranging my bedroom and there I found it hidden under the bed. An earring, a gold hoop. At first I thought it was mine, until I reached for it and realized it was attached to skin, crusted with blood. It had to have been Paulette's.

That night, without packing a bag, I ran out the house and drove to DC where Phoenix had flown in for a game. I stayed with him that night, where he held and tried to comfort me in his young arms. A year later those same arms were reaching out to me for other reasons, and somehow I felt obligated.

Then I met you, the first man to enter my home since Cole. What's more, you were the first to sleep in my bed. Trent, you had the ability to quell the ghosts. That first time your presence enabled me to sleep through the night, something I hadn't done since the tragedy.

But none of this is an excuse for how I deceived you; for the pain I caused. I love you, Trent, but I was scared. Scared to let go of the security that Phoenix provided because, by then, I was in trapped in a web of greed and some false allegiance.

Trent, I wanted so badly to be your wife. To be able to wipe my slate clean. To be a good woman and not live such a twisted life, but all that was taken away from me by my own hands. I have nobody to blame but myself.

I hope I haven't spoiled it for you, hope I haven't made it impossible for you to trust and love a woman again. You gave so much to me, that's why I left Phoenix – because I knew that you could provide me with a true reality but it was too late. I should've known that my secrets wouldn't last forever.

Having been with Phoenix cost me a lot. Not only have I lost my values, but more importantly, my sordid life has cost me you. It's not hard to understand or accept why I'll never hear from you again. I don't deserve a man like you. I just pray that one day your heart will soften in the places I've made hard. I broke the promise of my name; "Sasha, protector of men," because I couldn't protect the one man that truly loved me.

I love you Trent. Please take care of yourself and your heart and may you be blessed with a woman who truly deserves you.

Love always,

Sasha

EPILOGUE

SASHA

I'd been in St. Lucia for two weeks and as I lay on the beach waiting for Arshell to spend a week with me, I thought back over the past few years. What had I really learned from all this? And more importantly, what behavior would I not repeat? I'd made a mistake, hell I'd made a lot of mistakes but hadn't I paid for them.

A sudden sadness filled me as I realized what it meant to be alone, no Trent, no Phoenix, and no Cole. I knew Trent would never take me back but he did leave me a voicemail thanking me for the letter. Cole and I had finally closed the door on our relationship because we knew it would never pan out due to our past. And Phoenix, well, I prayed that I would never allow another man to hold me sexually hostage. Just today I'd seen him on the cover of *Fortune* magazine, an article on young millionaires and all I could look at was his lips. Damn, why did memories always just pop into your mind whenever they felt like it, then you have to torment yourself as to whether you lingered on them or not? So I lingered only for a few moments. And I thought about him. It wasn't a love affair we had. Just lust, just a need to please a man and him an ability to demand pleasure as often and from whomever he pleased. I just hoped there was someway I could salvage what was left of my emotions.

Going to therapy did seem to be helping, and it was my therapist who suggested I take a vacation. The therapist had assured me during our sessions, as she watched me spill over with emotions, that we'd get to the core of the reasons why I seemed to have not only a ravenous sexual appetite but also why I was emotionally insatiable. For me the two went together.

There was also the issue of losing my mother that I had to face that I'd never been able to admit. Thus, I'd never possessed some of life's relationship skills or knew the importance of one, that mothers were able to pass on to their daughters.

I had no idea what I'd do once I returned to Philly but I knew I'd be starting from scratch. Hell, I didn't even know if I'd stay in Philly, too many memories of too many men. But it didn't take away the fact that I hadn't had sex in about three months. There was no denying that I was starving for the touch of a man. I had been tempted while here but was trying to control myself by learning how to masturbate, which was giving me no relief. Then as I laid there on the beach tanning, I realized that the fine-ass man lying across from me, who was clearly with his wife, was smiling that familiar smile. As I turned to lay on my stomach, so he could have another view of me, I prayed that Arshell would hurry the hell up and arrive.